Cover Design: Missy Walker

Editor: Swish Design & Editing

BURNING RIVALRY

ELITE MEN OF LAS VEGAS BOOK #2

MISSY WALKER

For Nonna Connie, who taught me that good food takes time and love is always made by hand.

1

SEBASTIAN

Few things brought me more satisfaction than stepping into the kitchen before dawn—*my* kitchen, *my* restaurant, every detail tailored to my exacting standards. This was my world, my sanctuary. The only place I ever truly felt like myself. The king of my castle, soaking in the familiar aromas of recipes painstakingly developed or refactored, recipes that had built my reputation in a town—and an industry—notorious for breaking all but those with the strongest spirit. I hadn't been broken.

I had, however, been forced to bend.

Hence, the tight set of my jaw the morning my crew and I were set to meet our newest addition.

"We need her." My business manager's persistent, chiding voice rang out in my mind like a song I couldn't get rid of. Playing on repeat, ringing out the moment I opened my eyes in the week since Felix had

laid bare in front of me the facts of the situation. *"We need a name. We need a face people recognize."*

A sideshow. That was what my brand was going to turn into. After all these years, it was no longer about the recipes, the familiarity, or the sense of dining with family. It was about who could land a famous name to work in their kitchen—celebrity chefs—what a fucking joke. I had come up in their dawning age when cooking competitions had gotten their start and turned nobodies into overnight celebrities. The idea of a food blogger being given their own show on a major cable network still blew my mind. It was all viewed as entertainment ratings. Nobody was in it for the food, the tradition.

The clock had barely struck five when I unlocked the door and flipped on the lights, and as usual, I was the first to arrive. The kitchen gleamed, spotless after last night's service wrapped up. Lazy, half-assed behavior was not tolerated in my kitchen. I might not have gone to culinary school, but I'd made it my business to haunt the kitchens of chefs whose work I respected and whose reputations I wished to emulate. I had soaked up every drop of wisdom, staging in their kitchens as a sort of intern, getting my training on the job. There wasn't a smudge on any of the stainless-steel prep tables or a scuff mark on the tiled floor.

To walk in on such perfection was satisfying, knowing it would be destroyed by the end of the night but would be reset again for the morning.

Today was special. A different sort of destruction loomed ahead of me, not that it had to be so damn dramatic, but it felt that way as I entered my small office off the large pantry. By the time I'd put on a large pot of coffee for the crew and powered up my laptop to review last night's numbers, the sound of shuffling feet reached me. One by one, the kitchen staff members wandered in, some looking and sounding half asleep, carrying paper cups of coffee, yawning loudly, greeting each other once they left their things in their lockers. There was good-natured joking, along with the musical sound of pots and pans being removed from their hooks and shelves in preparation for the day's use. It was like a symphony playing out every day, starting at exactly this time.

It was a symphony about to be knocked out of sync thanks to a new musician stepping on stage.

I had to stop grinding my teeth if I didn't want to visit the dentist anytime soon. Claudia Granger. The fucking flash-in-the-pan winner of a televised cooking competition, somebody who believed she had any place in my kitchen. It was a fucking insult, plain and simple. My restaurant routinely made it to the top ten lists of favorite Vegas locations. We were praised for modern takes on classic dishes, providing consistently excellent food and service. Nobody around here was trying to reinvent the wheel, something our longtime patrons appreciated.

At least, they used to.

There went my teeth again, grinding together as I stepped out of my office and silently observed some of the activity going on as vegetables were chopped, butter clarified, and vegetable scraps being roasted for stock. *My* kitchen, *my* team. The delicate balance they had achieved was about to be destroyed.

My sous chef turned to me, opening one of the oven doors to stir the vegetable scraps roasting along with the bones that would eventually become an intensely flavorful reduction. "So what's the news?" Lucas asked, then returned to his checklist of items to be prepped. "When does the TV star get here?"

I had to fight back the reply that bubbled up in me. As far as I was concerned, she didn't have to arrive for her first day. I'd secretly hoped she wouldn't. Not that I wanted to fail, but it would have meant an excuse not to keep her here. There had to be a reason the girl couldn't get a job in New York, of all places. Why did she have to come way out here to find work when one couldn't swing a dead cat in Manhattan without hitting ten restaurants?

"Soon," I promised, my experienced eye moving over the prep stations. "Let's all give her time to adjust. I know none of you are a big fan of having her here."

Allie, one of the line cooks, turned my way in the middle of slicing a mountain of onions. "Speak for yourself, boss. I'll be glad to get a little more estrogen up in this place."

"Oh, please," Lucas groaned, elbowing Allie on his

way past. "I remember you saying you recorded all the episodes the season she was on because you knew from the beginning she was gonna win. Superfan alert."

"Whatever. I'm just trying to be a team player. You could take a lesson," she added, sticking her tongue out at him.

I had also watched the show. I made it my business after learning I was being forced to bring her in. Allie made a point—the girl was a star, somebody with charisma and talent combined. According to my internet search, she had been the fan favorite early on in the season, and her fame had only grown as the weeks went on.

A girl like her didn't belong here.

It wasn't the first time I had to remind myself not to use her behavior on the show as an indicator of how she would be in real life, always trying to put her special touch on tried-and-true recipes. She wanted to innovate and set herself apart. It was a cute idea that would not get her far around here. I knew what worked, and I'd built a brand on it.

If it worked, why do you have to bring her in?

I turned away from the team, scrubbing a hand over my dark hair. There was no turning away from the chiding, berating voice in my skull. "Let's give her a chance," I called out over my shoulder as the back door swung open, and a petite blonde walked in.

Never in my thirty-three years had I been taken

aback so completely. Immediately, my brain refused to accept what was in front of me. She couldn't have been more than five feet tall, wearing a button-down shirt, leggings, and thick-rimmed glasses, which made her bright blue eyes appear larger, almost putting them out of balance with the rest of her delicate face. Her golden blonde hair was clipped neatly at the nape of her neck, and from her shoulders hung the straps of a backpack roughly half her size. She could have been a kid on her way to school. If I had seen her from a distance, that's exactly what I would have assumed.

Her voice was strong, full of energy and confidence as she approached with one small hand outstretched. "Sebastian Kennedy, I take it?"

At first, I was too gobsmacked to respond. She looked bigger on television. Did they give her a box to stand on? *Get it together, asshole.* "That's me. And you must be Claudia Granger."

"That's right." She flashed the winning smile I had gazed down on while studying her portfolio put together by the PR genius, Sienna Black, back in New York. Claudia wasn't nearly as polished in person, but her smile was the same—brash, confident. "I'm so glad to meet you," she offered. "I'm looking forward to the opportunity to work together."

Meanwhile, the symphony that had been taking place behind me softened to near silence. If I had eyes in the back of my head, I would have no doubt found the crew watching while pretending not to. "We are also glad to have you here," I lied. The strangled snicker behind me developed into a soft chorus of barely stifled laughter.

In other words, this was going beautifully.

If she noticed the awkwardness, she ignored it, her smile remaining firmly in place as she took in our surroundings. "What a gorgeous kitchen. Would you like to show me around first, or should we sit down and discuss your expectations? I've brought a binder full of my recipes and photos. I would be so happy to work with you to put together a dessert menu that compliments your entrées."

Hitting the ground running. I couldn't hold it against her, though I was not in the habit of letting others dictate my process. I hadn't intended to jump in with both feet moments after her arrival. Standing in front of her, I had to wonder if she could hack it in a large, fast-paced kitchen like this one. The people standing behind me were hardened veterans, while she looked barely strong enough to lift the bowl of an industrial-size mixer.

"Please, let's go to my office," I offered, sweeping my arm in that direction. "I generally like to chat with potential new employees before hiring them, so you see I'm already a step behind in all this."

"It has been a little awkward, hasn't it?" She was doing her best to be cheerful, bright, and sunny like the persona she'd put across in a dozen talk show appearances since her win when she'd been crowned

America's Best Baker. Absolutely fucking ridiculous, meaningless, a so-called honor. For some reason, people took that sort of shit seriously. Hence, her presence.

This isn't all about you. It was about my employees, my legacy. There was a hell of a lot riding on this, and I couldn't afford to let my ego get in the way, or so I'd been told by Felix. It was easy for him to say.

"Between you and me, I have so looked forward to sitting down with you and picking your brain." She stood in the doorway to my cramped office. I didn't notice until I sat at my desk how uncertain she looked.

"Is there a problem?" I asked, gesturing toward a small, padded chair near mine.

Her eyelashes fluttered as she released a soft chuckle. "I'm sorry. I expected something... bigger. That sounds all wrong, doesn't it?" Yes, my office probably seemed downright miniature compared to the offices of major network producers.

"I would rather have as much space as possible devoted to work outside this room," I explained while she took a seat, immediately setting her backpack on the floor and unzipping it to pull out a binder stuffed with pages. Neon-colored Post-it notes stuck out here and there. It looked like she'd spilled coffee on it at one point, some of the pages discolored and wavy at the edges.

"I get the feeling we're going to get along just fine," she assured me with a soft laugh. "I would be the same way. It's just, with a reputation like yours, I imagined you would splurge on a larger office. Goes to show how much I know, right?"

It went to show how little experience she had in a real, working kitchen. "Well, I imagine you're used to working in cramped spaces too. TV cameras and lighting rigs must take up a lot of room."

Her blue eyes flicked away from my framed certificates and awards on the wall behind me, her brows drawing together over the rims of those ridiculous glasses. "Pardon me?"

"I'm just saying. TV sets. I'm sure there can't be much room when you have all that equipment around you."

She crossed her legs, balanced the open binder across them, then folded her arms. "I've done much more than that." The bright, sunny voice had gone flat. If anything, it was an improvement. Who was genuinely that chipper at six in the morning? "Exactly how much do you know about me?"

I sat up straighter, matching her energy, noting the twitching in the apple of her cheek. It didn't take much to set her off, though she was doing all she could to conceal it. "Sienna provided a thorough portfolio covering your training and experience," I explained, now more cordial to counter her iciness.

"So you realize I trained in France? Not to mention the year I spent in New York before the competition?"

Inclining my head, I murmured, "I'm well aware and impressed."

"I didn't ask," she muttered, clamping her mouth shut over eyes that widened like she hadn't meant to let that slip.

This conversation was going nowhere, and every word I said only made it worse. The entire situation wasn't my style, which was probably a large part of the problem—kissing ass, playing nice, layering lies between us for the sake of making it work. I prided myself on being upfront, sometimes almost brutally honest. There was no room for ass-kissing in this industry.

Rather than continue the charade a minute longer, I decided to lay my cards on the table. "Claudia, let's clear the air. I had no desire to hire you because I don't think a famous name aligns with the brand I've worked so hard to build over the past decade. As far as I'm concerned, this is a charade intended to—"

"Refresh the brand you've worked so hard to build over the past decade?" she suggested while looking me up and down, almost like it was for the first time. "Sebastian, from where I'm sitting, your brand is in danger. Your reservation book is not as full as it used to be, and your waiting list? It's practically nonexistent. Tell me I'm wrong."

Before I could force a word out of my mouth, she added, "Sienna was very thorough when it came to researching you, as well. I don't walk into situations I'm unaware of," she explained, her fingertips tapping the first page in her binder in a slow, deliberate rhythm. "We both know what this is about. You need me, and I need work. Why don't we skip the part where we blow smoke up each other's asses and express our undying gratitude and get right to work. I have a lot to do."

My pride reared, demanding satisfaction. "Exactly why couldn't you find work in New York?" I asked, noting the way her face fell slightly. "I mean, with a sparkling personality like the one you've displayed so far, I'd think restaurant owners would be beating down your door."

"That's my business," she replied, practically looking down her nose at me.

"Working with a brand you so blithely disparaged? That's your business?"

Her eyes narrowed slightly. "Yes, it is. I not only needed work, I needed a new start. That's all I'm going to say."

Fair enough.

But if she thought I would kiss her feet for deigning to work with me, she had another thing coming.

2

CLAUDIA

Well, so much for keeping things positive and friendly on my first day.

Not like it was my fault. The arrogant, sanctimonious prick had the nerve to disparage me within the first five minutes of our acquaintance. What! Was I supposed to sit there and let him insult me? What was that crack about the television cameras supposed to be about?

He even managed to look surprised as he blinked hard, a small smile tipping the corners of his mouth like he was trying to decide if this was a joke. No, the joke was this tiny little office and the ragtag crew of jokers out there who didn't bother hiding their laughter when I came in. Was I supposed to get the warm fuzzies after going through that? Was I supposed to feel welcome in my new place of business?

"You know how these types of guys are." Sienna

Black had done her best to warn me, hadn't she? "Decent people, nice in general, but they tend to think the moon and stars were hung for them, according to their specifications. Sometimes, it's a matter of letting them think they're getting their way. You'll be able to handle him with no problem."

In other words, smile and go along with it. Not exactly something I had ever been good at.

Which led to this situation—sitting in a tiny little room with a very tall, muscular man who stared at me like I was some species he hadn't yet become familiar with. His steely gray eyes narrowed as they moved over me while his sharp jaw ticked. He wasn't bad to look at, but that was about the only good thing I could come up with as I waited for him to form a response.

Finally, he did, tipping his head back and looking at me over the bridge of his nose. "Well, I wouldn't want to hold you up, being as important as you are. I'm sure you have all kinds of ideas about how you want to change things up around here since you're already so well-versed in the needs of my brand. Please, tell me everything. What did you have in mind?"

The tiniest part of me, so small it wouldn't have shown up under a microscope, wished I hadn't started this. I shouldn't have said it, but he had dropped the first blow. Not that it mattered, not that it would do me any favors if I accused him of that. I would only come off hopelessly childish if I started pointing fingers at the age of twenty-eight.

Instead, I decided to take his question at face value and offer an honest answer, though I was careful to choose one that wouldn't immediately antagonize him. "You've had some trouble," I offered, and even my voice was different—a little softer, more understanding. No matter how good I knew I was, I needed this job. I needed to prove to the culinary world I was more than a one-trick pony, and working with Sebastian Kennedy was a great place to start.

In other words, I needed to play nice. "You had those weird allegations of food poisoning a couple of months back. People started talking about whether you had run your course. Unfortunately, by then, you had already sunk a ton of time and money into a second location on the opposite end of the Strip. It was already too late to back out, not that you would back out if you could," I added, sprinkling a little editorializing on top of the facts.

Naturally, he picked up on it right away, like a shark smelling blood in the water. It was surprising his eyes didn't roll back to reveal the whites. "What makes you say that?" he asked.

"Because I wouldn't, either," I admitted. "Listen, you don't get as far as you have in this business or in any business if you're the type of person who rolls over and plays dead at the first sign of adversity. Besides, by then, it was no secret you were expanding. If you gave up, it would mean having to explain to people why you had given up, and you wouldn't want to do that any more than I would."

He didn't like being so easily read. Shifting his weight in his chair, he tightened his jaw, narrowed his eyes, and basically played the part of the intimidating boss. "I'm glad you think we have so much in common, and I appreciate your attempt at understanding." He barely stopped short of rolling his eyes, and I instantly regretted trying to relate to him. Some people weren't worth the trouble, and he was proving himself to be one of them.

Rather than give me a chance to retort, he kept rolling, again shifting his weight and making the chair squeak as a result. I really had expected him to sit in a much nicer office. Couldn't he afford a better chair?

"You were right on several counts, but then you know that." God, he was resentful, almost biting off his words. His mouth hardly moved when he spoke, and the effect was unnerving. "Yes, we've had some trouble. There was a time I was convinced someone was deliberately sabotaging me, though I was never able to find any evidence to support that theory." His gaze went unfocused for a moment as he stared over my shoulder, looking back at the recent past and sounding murderous. I probably would too.

He snapped back to the present, flexing his long fingers and running one hand through dark brown waves just disheveled enough to be alluring. It was the sort of hair a girl wondered about—*would it be as soft and thick as it looked?* Not that I wanted to run my fingers through it unless the goal was to rip it out of his head for snarking at me.

"It seemed that overnight, I went from enjoying a sterling reputation to asking myself what the hell could possibly happen next," he continued, unaware of how I imagined a big bald spot on his head. "Constant issues with the plumbing, rumors of unsanitary conditions, and a surprise health inspection which we nearly failed for some unknown reason. It was never made clear what the problem was," he grunted. "We were given a warning. That was the first time in my career such a thing had happened. It all started with the torrent of shit reviews stating our food gave customers food poisoning."

He offered a dry, humorous chuckle. "Like I said, I was convinced we were being sabotaged, but whoever was behind it was clever enough to hide their involvement."

"Do you have enemies around here?" His eyebrows nearly left his forehead when they shot up all at once, and this time, I felt the need to apologize. "Sometimes I say the first thing that comes to my head without thinking about it."

"No kidding. I had no idea." He rolled his eyes, and I did the same.

"But I think I deserve to know if the man whose restaurant I'm baking for has people out there wanting to cut his throat," I added.

Scoffing, he replied, "I wouldn't use the word enemies."

So, the answer is yes.

"Competitors, certainly," he continued. "Only the guy with nothing going for him can walk through without detractors. The guy who's not a threat to anyone. That has never been me," he insisted with pride in his voice. Was I supposed to congratulate him?

"There's something we have in common," I offered instead. It wasn't much, but it was something.

The flash of his smile was like light gleaming off a sharpened knife. "Is that why you couldn't get a job in New York?"

This motherfucker. To think, there I was, trying to smooth things over. All I had done was respond to his hostility. I tried to make up for that, and what happened? He had to take another fucking dig. How was I supposed to work with a person like this?

The worst part? He didn't look remotely sorry. Not so much as an attempt at an apology. Because he knew me so well, right? He thought he caught me in a 'gotcha' moment, the prick. Maybe he expected me to run away in tears. I'd already done more than enough of that lately.

"As a matter of fact, I recently accepted an offer in New York." Pausing to take a breath, I added, "However, we had a falling out. After that, I was free to accept this position."

Don't ask about it.

Do. Not.

The hand resting on my binder clenched, my nails digging into my palm. What little there was of them sank into my flesh, flesh that had long since become accustomed to pain—searing ovens, hot pans, spills, accidents. My hands were a roadmap detailing every step of my journey over the years.

It was only recently that my internal pain began.

Do not ask.

Do. Not.

I wasn't sure what I would do if he dug around for more information. I waited for a snarky comeback, a seemingly innocent question with invisible barbs.

When he only grunted softly, my hand relaxed a little. With the raw and unfiltered mood I was in, I might have done something unforgivable, like describe the humiliation of discovering my fiancé fucking my would-be employer in *my* bed. That was the worst part—deeper than the humiliation, sharper than the betrayal. They did it in *my* bed, a bed I had purchased and shared with him after he moved in.

I was supposed to be planning a wedding and beginning a new career in Manhattan. Instead, I was in Las Vegas, of all places, in the middle of the desert. I already missed autumn in New York, where there actually felt like a change in seasons. I missed my life.

There might have been seasons in New York, but there was also Brandon and all the promises he'd made and broken. The twenty-five hundred miles between us hardly seemed like enough when I reflected on his wandering dick.

"What are your goals?" Sebastian asked, forcing me to tamp down my murderous thoughts in the interest of keeping a job I hadn't asked for but felt forced to take.

It came out before common sense could stop me. "I want to work at a Michelin Star restaurant."

He might have tried not to laugh, looking almost constipated at first, but lost the battle. "Well, put that on your list to Santa Claus this year, and we'll see what he can do for you." He chortled, the asshole. He actually chortled.

"Is that funny somehow?" I asked, my head tipping to the side. "Because I fail to see the humor."

"No? Let me explain." He folded his hands over his flat stomach, drawing my attention to his lips when he pursed them. Nice lips, a little pouty. What a shame they belonged to this absolute asshole. "Chasing a star is like chasing a tiger. You manage to grab its tail, then you ask yourself what the hell you're going to do with it."

What, did somebody tell you that? Because he certainly had never earned one of his own. I wasn't suicidal—the words never left my mouth. No matter how I felt about his posturing, I needed the work. And despite his attitude and recent downturn, he had a solid reputation out here.

"I'll take my chances." I decided with a grin.

A grin he did not return. “Not here, you won’t.”

Somewhere in my head, a needle scratched a record. Loudly. “Pardon?”

“My kitchen isn’t where you’ll experiment and stretch your limits in pursuit of an empty award, which I promise will not make you as happy as you think it will.” My mouth fell open in disbelief, but he decided to keep going. “The recipes used in this restaurant and the new location once it opens, draw from generations of tradition in my family. I refuse to sign a paycheck for someone who views this position as a training ground for what they ultimately want.”

“So you expect someone to recreate the same recipes week in and week out?” I asked, still finding it difficult to believe. When he nodded, I asked, “Why not hire a trained monkey if that’s all you’re looking for?”

“Did the trained monkey win a cooking competition?”

A sharp pain lodged itself in my stomach. That was a low blow. Nothing about him changed to reveal regret over taking such a cheap shot. “We need each other,” he concluded, his cheek twitching beneath a thin layer of dark scruff. “Let’s keep that in mind as you learn the ropes around here. I’d advise you to familiarize yourself with the current seasonal dessert rotation and the typical bread service in the restaurant. Lucas can give you a hand with that.”

Which one is Lucas? He didn’t bother explaining

further. I didn't ask. I would have rather chewed glass than ask. "Sounds good." I slid my binder into the backpack at my feet without saying another word about it, but that in no way meant he'd won. Not even close.

I'd bide my time for now, learn the ropes, and earn the respect of the crew now working happily and efficiently in the kitchen.

Then, I'd make Sebastian Kennedy look like the talentless hack he was by showing his loyal customers what they'd been missing out on all along.

3

SEBASTIAN

"So then, I asked the pink elephant if he wanted a ride in my car, but he said there was no room. I guess I should upgrade to a pickup or something like that."

I nodded slowly in response to Aiden's story, only a few words of which had filtered into my consciousness so far. Something about wanting to buy a new car? It didn't matter. My gaze remained trained where it had been since sitting at one of the tables in my dining room—on the large window in the door leading back to the kitchen, where I could occasionally find a golden head bobbing as its owner moved back and forth. What the hell was she doing?

"So instead, he offered me a ride on his back." Finally, a slap against my arm stirred my attention. I scowled at my friend, Aiden McConnell, before the stupidity of what he had just said sank in. Vaughn Eastman and Grayson Daniels chuckled while I looked around the table. “What the hell are you all talking about?” I asked, resulting in more laughter.

“I’m glad you finally started listening because I’m not sure how much longer I could have gone on with that story. Where the hell is your mind?” Aiden asked, tapping a finger against the side of his head and laughing as he sat back with his drink.

“Hey, guys. Sorry I’m late.” Jackson Bennett joined us, dropping into the fifth chair around the table and brushing his overgrown blond hair away from his forehead. Now that he was in town on a long-term contract with a few of the casinos, we made it a point to invite him to join us when he had the chance. “What did I miss?” he asked after flirting his way through a drink order.

“Not much,” Vaughn told him, snorting. “Aiden was telling a story to see whether Sebastian over here was ever going to pay attention.”

“So far...” Aiden concluded, “... he’s too busy obsessing over his new pastry chef.”

“Watch it,” I warned, painfully aware of the number of guests who’d shown up tonight to see her like they had the past two evenings. Word sure got around quickly. “That’s not funny.”

“What are you so touchy about tonight?” Grayson asked without the laughter edging Aiden’s voice. “Are things not working out? She’s only been here, what, a few days?”

“The longest days of my career,” I confirmed. There

wasn't an antacid strong enough to calm the burning discomfort whenever I thought of her. The mere thought of her name left me rubbing my chest.

"You okay?" Vaughn wasn't joking, setting his glass down and giving me a look of concern. "We shouldn't have done this here tonight. This is supposed to be when we get together and unwind. All you can do is worry over what's happening in the kitchen." Now that he and his accidental wife, Nova, had ironed things out and were blissfully happy, he saw himself in a position to offer advice to the rest of us.

"How's the new show shaping up?" Aiden asked Jackson, trying to be helpful and change the subject. For once, I could appreciate him being able to bounce from one topic to the next like an overstimulated toddler.

"One of my principal dancers dropped out today because she fell in love and is moving to Wichita. I wish I were joking." He unceremoniously dumped a glass of whiskey down his throat, tapping it, and handed it back to the server for a refill. "Sorry to send you right back, but I'm thirsty tonight." Rubbing his temples, he squeezed his amber eyes shut.

"Imagine. She would rather move to Kansas than work with you," Aiden quipped, and even I could laugh.

"Don't get me wrong, she tried getting in my pants..." he informed us once the laughter died down, "... when she was first cast. Like that would get her somewhere. I'm sick of women who think they can throw themselves at you to get ahead."

That was one thing I could say Claudia had not so much as approached—quite the opposite. Whenever we ran into each other in the kitchen, she made it a point to look at me like a rodent had run across her foot. Granted, I felt pretty much the same toward her, so there were no hurt feelings.

Vaughn caught me looking through the window again and chuckled. "Why don't you just go back there and get it over with? It's where you would rather be."

"Yeah, we won't take it personally," Grayson assured me.

"Speak for yourself. My friend invites me to his restaurant for dinner and drinks, and I expect a little hospitality." Aiden nudged my ankle under the table. "So? Be hospitable."

"I would, but I'm a hundred miles away," I grumbled. "Honestly, she is much more trouble than she's worth."

"Oh, the new girl? The one who was on TV?" When I nodded, Jackson whistled softly. "She's hot, at least. It can't be bad to have her to look at in the kitchen."

"Says the man who routinely complains about the dancers he watches all day long," Grayson reminded him.

"When they're fucking around with your career in

their hands, they're not so hot anymore, are they?" I asked.

Jackson nodded while accepting his second drink, which he sipped this time. "That's true."

"Are things that serious?" Grayson looked concerned.

"If she keeps trying to go behind my back to, you know, realize her *vision*?" I formed air quotes around the word and did my best not to gag. "Yeah, it's serious."

"Exactly what has she done?" Vaughn asked.

I almost wished he wouldn't. His curiosity came from a good place, as the others did, but knowing that did nothing to ease the tightness in my chest and the buzzing in my head. "It's not so much what she's done as what she's talked about," I explained. "She has this enormous binder full of recipes she wanted to show me. She wants to develop new recipes to make her mark on *my* restaurant. She thinks that's going to earn her a Michelin Star," I concluded with a laugh. "She doesn't have the first idea."

"You've gotta be pretty innovative to get one of those, don't you?" Jackson mused. "Like, really out-there and experimental. That's not what you do here."

"Thank you!" Maybe I said it a little too loudly—the bartender and a handful of well-dressed patrons sitting at the bar looked my way. I lowered the hands I'd thrown into the air and released a deep breath.

"Thank you," I murmured once I'd calmed myself.

"Maybe you should go back there and explain that to her because while I tried to explain it myself, I kept overhearing her talking about things she wants to try. I am not interested in her trying anything. She is here for her name, and that is all."

"You sure as hell seem pretty busy around here," Grayson observed, eyeing the busy room with its criss-crossing servers. He wasn't wrong. We were booked solid again, and a cursory glance around the packed dining room revealed more than a few guests craning their necks, trying to get a glimpse of what went on in the kitchen—in other words, trying to get a glimpse of her, hoping to get a selfie.

"Fucking sideshow," I muttered, shaking my head bitterly. "That's all it is."

"Isn't that the whole gimmick here in Vegas?" Jackson pointed out with a good-natured grin. "Get them through the door using a name, make them stay, and give you their money once you offer value."

"He's right," Aiden agreed. "She's the draw. She's bringing people in for you and creating a buzz about the new restaurant in advance of its opening. That can only be a good thing."

None of them got it. The more I pushed, the less they would understand. "I'm sure you're right," I muttered, biting back my bitterness for the sake of changing the topic.

Unfortunately, no such thing was possible since the

kitchen door swung open, and the woman of the hour stepped out.

I was going to be sick.

Instantly, a barrage of cell phones emerged, all held up so their owners could capture footage of Claudia offering a brief wave to the people who had clearly assembled in hopes of meeting her. The woman framed in the doorway was miles from the woman who had first entered my kitchen—polished, smiling, her glasses ditched in favor of contacts, her face made up.

It was a shame she looked so damn good.

"She's smaller in real life than she was on TV," Aiden mused. When I arched an eyebrow, he shrugged. "What? I saw her on a show last time I was at the doctor's office. They had it playing in the waiting room."

"Please." Grayson chuckled. "I bet you were on the message boards, rooting for her to win the competition."

"Cute," Jackson murmured with obvious approval in his voice. "Very."

"Don't be fooled," I warned through my teeth. For the sake of show, I maintained a pleasant expression, especially when Claudia passed our table.

"Sebastian," she murmured, smiling warmly as she took in the faces of the men assembled around me. "Are these the friends I heard were visiting you tonight?"

What the fuck did she know about it? One thing about working in the kitchen—word intended to spread quickly. Not that there was anything inherently wrong with her knowing my friends would visit, but the idea of there being chatter surrounding my life didn't sit well with me.

"Yes, these are my special guests tonight." I made the introductions and watched her shake their hands while a few giggling young women seated nearby took photos and videos. My skin prickled, and my collar felt too tight like it was strangling me. What else could I do but sit back and play the part of the affable restaurateur?

Vaughn cleared his throat before sliding a guilty glance my way. "Would you mind taking a photo with me? My wife would love it. She's watched the entire season of your show and is a big fan."

"I'd be happy to." She crouched beside him and smiled brightly while Vaughn took a selfie on his phone, then thanked her for her time.

"It's my pleasure," she assured him. Our eyes locked briefly before her gaze drifted away, but there was enough in that look to rouse my irritation. She knew I hated this. She had to know I had made it clear. None of this was my idea. "I'm sure if you gentlemen are hungry, they could rustle up something nice for you in the kitchen."

"I'm sure I can handle it, thank you," I interjected.

"Whatever you say. You're the boss." She somehow

managed to make it sound like an insult before moving on and greeting more of her fans.

Aiden blew out a soft whistle, settling back in his chair. "I don't know how much work I'd get done with her around. Damn."

"For once, could you not think with your dick?" I muttered, watching her, gauging her progress from the corner of my eye. She played the part so well, carefully answering questions while accepting the adoration thrown so generously her way with an earnestness that made me want to jump to my feet and tell everyone within earshot range they needed to get their priorities straight. She won a fucking cooking show. That didn't mean she wasn't about to walk on water anytime soon.

"You know what you need?" Vaughn decided. "A visit to Dante's club. Work out some of your stress." We had all invested in Dante West's Vegas expansion and had visited more than once, indulging in the safety and anonymity the club provided. It wouldn't exactly be a good idea for any of us to openly show our faces there since we were all men with reputations in this town, but Dante believed in discretion above all things.

It was an appealing idea, but it didn't excite me the way it normally would. "I have too much to do," I decided, getting up from the table when Claudia finished her tour of the dining room. "Everyone ready to eat? I'll send a server over here," I told them, heading for the kitchen before anyone could respond.

It was time to talk about expectations, starting with this nightly sideshow.

The energy in the kitchen was hectic as ever, with voices overlapping and questions being called out. "Surprise additions on table five! I just put in another two filets, medium-rare!" one of the servers called out as she finished assembling a bread basket, adding a trio of small ramekins to the tray.

"Hang on. What is this?" I picked one of the ramekins, holding them up for inspection. Seasoned olive oil. "Since when? This isn't part of our bread service."

"Claudia added it tonight." The girl looked like she was ready to shit herself, trembling in the face of my anger. "I already had two tables rave about it."

"Each version is meant to compliment the three types of bread sent to the table." The sudden appearance of Claudia at my elbow was unwelcome, to say the least, even if she was the person who most deserved my aggravation. Pointing to them one at a time, she explained, "Black olive focaccia, sundried tomato sourdough, rosemary sea salt."

It was a small deviation. Some would say not worth getting pissed off about, but some people were not me, and I had every fucking reason to be exactly that. "Maybe you didn't get the memo," I growled, keeping my voice low while the server scurried off with the tray. "But you do *not* make changes like that without consulting me. Frankly, I don't see how you have the time..." I added with a smirk, "... with all the selfies you've been part of the past few days."

Most people would openly avoid openly rolling their eyes. She was not most people. "Oh, you mean when I was busy playing the part of the gracious celebrity chef?"

"Celebrity chef?" I almost choked on my tongue. "Do us both a favor and never call yourself that again. You sound ridiculous."

A deep red, angry flush crept up her neck and spread across her face. "I forgot. You've already cornered the market on sounding ridiculous in this kitchen."

Someone in the kitchen let out a long, high-pitched whistle in response to that. The sound snapped me back to the reality of the situation, and the same seemed to be true for her. Her eyelids fluttered, she lowered her head and trembled as she stared at my feet. "I have guests to attend to," I choked out, fighting for every breath before pushing the swinging door open. They would see right away how flustered I'd become, no doubt, and would probably give me shit for it.

Instead, back at my table, Jackson held up a piece of focaccia glistening with olive oil. "This is the perfect pairing. I could make a meal out of this."

Claudia hadn't uttered another syllable, yet somehow, she'd gotten the last word.

And there wasn't a damn thing I could do about it.

4

CLAUDIA

It wasn't bad enough he had to be a complete jackass. No, he had to insult me in front of the entire kitchen. The kitchen that had gone somewhat quiet and still when moments ago it was full of frenetic activity.

The worst part was how he stared at me—defiant, nasty, daring me to talk back as if he wished I would give him a reason to fire me. And it would have been so easy to give him that reason too. After a handful of days in this kitchen, I had come up with more than a few observations he wouldn't have been very happy to hear. They could live in my back pocket until the time came to drop them on his head.

Be the bigger person. How many times had I heard that during the course of the show? Twelve weeks spent keeping my thoughts to myself, staying quiet when there were obvious injustices going on. What would all those people out there in the dining room think if they heard about the quiet, secretive sabotage that went on behind the scenes? When the producers decided which members of the group helped the ratings and which didn't. That mysteriously broken oven? Missing ingredients? They were not accidents.

Somehow, I had made the cut, but it was all hollow in the end. The win was supposed to be a stepping stone or a springboard to something bigger for me.

And this was something bigger?

Getting berated in front of my coworkers?

All I could do was shake. That, and be glad there was nothing sharp within an arm's reach, or that conversation might have gone a whole lot differently.

I was going to quit. I had to quit. There was still enough in my savings to float me for a little while until I found another job. A better job, with a better boss, one who wasn't completely psycho about everything staying exactly the same. No wonder the damn restaurant hadn't actually grown or evolved beyond its original concept—modern twists on classic dishes. Whoop-dee-fucking-doo.

Big, frustrated tears filled my eyes. There were two articles I was supposed to be interviewing for in the next couple of days, both of which pertained to my new position and how my presence would shake up the Strip. Something about leaving other pastry chefs shaking in their clogs, not that I would ever come up with a line as corny as that or put anyone else on alert that I was in town, gunning for their jobs.

Not even close. I wasn't out of my mind, looking to piss people off. I wasn't born and raised here, but I knew a thing or two. People relied on each other. And unlike the man whose name was on the sign out front, I didn't take an enemy's animosity as a sign of success. I got what he was going for, but his approach was all wrong. There was no need to piss people off to get ahead.

"Don't let him get to you."

Shit. I turned, sniffling, to find Lucas wearing a sympathetic expression. His dark eyes were soft, the corners of his mouth pulling downward. "He's tough, but so are you. And I like your bread," he added, coming to a stop and leaning against the prep table currently bearing my weight. For a big, sharp-tongued guy, when things were going wrong in the kitchen, he struck me as being surprisingly kind.

Standing up straight, I replied, "Thank you. I don't usually let anybody get to me that way."

"You're in a new place, a new job, a new kitchen. But everybody's been treating you pretty well, right?" he asked like he was trying to encourage me. I almost told him not to bother, it was a lost cause, but then again, I couldn't remember the last time anybody went out of their way to be nice the way he was now. He didn't have to. He was a busy guy in a busy kitchen, keeping the gears turning while his boss joked around with buddies and got all the praise.

"Everybody here has been decent," I assured him,

arching an eyebrow. "You wouldn't have anything to do with that, would you?"

His fair cheeks darkened. "What do you mean?" He turned back to his work plating entrées, but not quickly enough to hide the slight grin that had started to stir.

And there I was, letting myself believe I wasn't being hazed because everybody around here had respect for me. Or that at least this was too busy a professional kitchen for anyone to have the time. "I can take care of myself, you know," I murmured. "Thank you if you told them to lay off. It's been sort of a... crazy situation lately."

"Tell me about it. It's been crazy here too." Eyeing me up, he added, "You're supposed to turn all that around. So far, so good, at least from where I'm standing."

There was something in his words that gave me pause. Maybe it was the way he said it—a little too approving, maybe a little too familiar. But the way I was feeling, I welcomed it. I had an ally in the kitchen.

Make that two. "He can be such a hard-ass sometimes," Allie whispered as she approached. Raising her voice, she called out, "Behind you." Lucas was careful to avoid a collision.

"He's stuck in his ways," Lucas agreed, pushing up his sleeve when it fell across his forearm. The many tattoos were fascinating. "You just keep doing what you do. And remember, you've always got a taste tester right here if you want to try out a new project."

"I'll keep you in mind," I promised. By the time I returned to my corner of the kitchen, I had pushed back the tears, locking my emotions behind a steel door in favor of getting a rundown from my assistant, Stella, a middle-aged woman with a tart tongue and no problems telling off anybody who made the mistake of screwing with her. There was nothing but love among the crew, though tensions could run high at times.

"We're fine through the rest of tonight's service," she explained, then went on her break. I reviewed the list of desserts we were offering—tiramisu, chocolate cake with ganache frosting, and apple tart with cinnamon ice cream, a seasonal offering playing on traditional apple pie.

Boring. All of it.

Delicious? Sure.

Add enough butter, sugar, and chocolate to just about anything, and it was possible to make a really delicious dessert. But having looked through the books and done the required work to identify the supplies being ordered for these and other desserts left me with a pretty stark understanding—not enough people were ordering another course after their meals.

Why? I had a theory. It wasn't worth the money and the calories if the result wasn't spectacular. Sure, there were plenty of people up and down the Strip who would gorge themselves on anything remotely tasty-looking, but this wasn't some cheap buffet. People who dined here were a little more sophisticated, a little savvier. *Home by Sebastian Kennedy* was known for its warm, classic dishes, not for a stellar dessert menu.

I could change that. I knew I could. Just thinking about the recipes clogging my binder made my heart ache. I'd really fooled myself into thinking I would have a chance here, but my hopes were just about diminished.

Rather than give in, I rolled up my sleeves and began working on pastry crusts for tomorrow's apple tarts. The shells were parbaked, then finished once the dish was ordered by filling them with chopped, cooked apples in a sweet and slightly tangy sauce.

Predictable. Average at best.

Rather than go through the motions of preparing the crust based on the recipe, I rummaged around in the cool room and found a block of gruyere, of which I cut a piece to grate into the dough. It was hardly revolutionary, but it was a step up from the bland and predictable version that had been served here for far too long.

Slowly going through the motions of preparing the dough calmed me—grating the cheese, working cold butter into the flour. I lost myself to the rhythm of the work, reflecting on how I would have killed for the privilege of doing this back when I was a kid when every cent counted, and the idea of using precious resources for experiments was beyond insane. *Unthink-*

able. How many mornings had I watched Mom scrape the thinnest pat of butter imaginable over a piece of toast? How many mornings had she gone hungry or drank her coffee black because there was only enough milk for one of us to have cereal?

And here I was, grating pricy cheese into a tart crust made with European butter.

I had come a long way.

But there was so much farther I wanted to go.

Rolling out the dough, I cut away enough for a single, individual-size tart and pressed it into the mold, pricking it all over with a fork and sliding it into the oven. "What's that for?" Stella asked when she returned from her break, and I pulled the shell from the oven. By now, the others were waiting in the refrigerator, set to be used tomorrow night.

"Just a little something I've been thinking about." I looked to the left, then the right, then held a finger to my lips. "Don't tell the big, bad boss," I whispered. "Wouldn't want to get in trouble."

"It smells amazing." She stood back and watched while I fried sliced apples and pears together in a pan, having browned the butter first to add a nutty flavor and a deeper richness. The apples I'd used were slightly tart and the pears were sweet, meaning the flavors would play off each other in the finished dish.

"You'll have to test it for me," I offered, smiling with her eyes lit up.

"You know how he feels about the apple tart," she

warned just the same. "It was hard enough to convince him he didn't need to serve actual pies just because they were what his grandmother made." He needed to let go of the obsession he had with tradition. Of course, there was room for it, but not if somebody wanted to make a name for themselves.

Rather than leave the tart as it was once I filled the shell, I sprinkled finishing sugar on top, then placed it under the broiler for a few minutes until a nice caramelization bubbled on the surface. When it was finished, I left it out to cool before adding a scoop of cinnamon ice cream on top. We watched, both of us smiling dreamily as the ice cream began to melt.

"Help yourself," I offered, handing her a spoon and waiting while she managed to get a mouthful that included all three elements.

I then watched her eyes close once she took that first bite. "Oh, sweet baby Jesus," she whispered. "The brown butter? Genius. And what is that in the crust? There's something different."

"Gruyere," I confirmed.

"That's incredible." She tapped her chin, narrowing her dark eyes. "Do you know what you should do? You should make it just like this tomorrow night."

"Tomorrow night?" What was tomorrow night?

"Oh, it's family dinner night," she explained and took another bite. "He has his whole family come in twice a month for a big dinner... parents, sister, aunts, and uncles. And his nonna," she concluded.

Nonna, whose recipes were law, never amended, never to be trifled with. "Nice people?" I asked, though I found it hard to believe they would be. If so, how had somebody like him resulted?

"Oh, the sweetest," she replied, groaning softly. "You should make this tomorrow. For her. Don't tell him in advance."

The woman was a mind reader. "We'll see," I decided, though my mind had been made up before she said a word.

5

SEBASTIAN

"Where is she?" My sister, Maddie, craned her neck, trying to get a glimpse inside the kitchen, when the doors swung open as servers passed through in both directions.

"Young lady, you are going to give yourself neck strain if you don't give it a rest." Mom shook her head in mock disapproval, exchanging a grin with my Aunt Laura. "Would you believe me if I told you she hasn't stopped talking about this for days?"

I loved my baby sister. I usually indulged her youthful exuberance, but she was testing me tonight. Not that it was her fault. I was sick to death of hearing about the woman who was supposed to be my salvation, but up to this point, she had offered nothing but chronic heartburn. "She's doing her job," I told Maddie, giving her long, brown braid a quick tug because I knew it irritated her. Here I was, thirty-three years old, still determined to irritate my little sister. Then again, our age gap had made it difficult to spend a lot of time together when we were at the age when brothers and sisters normally antagonized each other for sport. Fifteen years was a big difference.

She flipped her braid to the other shoulder, where I couldn't reach it, giving me the sort of withering look only an eighteen-year-old could manage. "Duh, obviously. I just want to get a look at her. Can you get her to come out and say hi?"

"Madison Marie, that is enough," Mom declared, looking to Dad for guidance. Everyone knew when the full name came out, all bets were off.

"You heard your mother," Dad offered, enough to make Maddie snarl at me and return to the lasagna on her plate.

Aunt Laura passed a plate of garlicky greens around the table. "But really, how is it going? Are the two of you getting along?"

Uncle Matteo, my mom's brother, wiggled his eyebrows almost suggestively. "Does she have one of those TV diva personalities?" he asked in a loud, conspiratorial whisper.

"You promised you wouldn't ask a question like that," Aunt Laura grumbled, elbowing him, but he didn't seem penitent.

"It's not a prying question. Don't tell me you haven't wondered," he retorted.

"Things are going fine," I told them, knowing the

alternative would only destroy their illusions and might very well lead to even more discomfort in the form of additional questions, suggestions, and well-meaning advice I had *not* asked for. That was the way of life in a family.

"What do you think of the calamari, Nonna?" I asked my grandmother, sitting in the place of honor at the head of the table, as always. She'd once told me she looked forward to these family dinners more than just about anything, which meant they'd become a tradition. She had spent enough years of her life feeding all of us, after all. "Is it crispy enough for you?"

"You tell that girl at the fryer she has the touch of an angel," Nonna declared before snagging another crispy, breaded ring. It was her favorite dish, meaning we always placed the platter in front of her to give her first dibs. The sight of her gnarled hands, thin-skinned and delicate, warmed and chilled my heart at the same time. How many Sundays had I spent in her kitchen, sitting at the table, watching her knead dough and roll out homemade pasta? I had studied her gentle, practiced touch, and marveled at the magic those hands created.

They didn't used to look so old. Now, they were still strong but delicate. Her once lustrous chocolate-brown hair was now a silver mass pinned in a knot at the nape of her neck. Time could be cruel.

"Maddie, how is everything going these last few months of school?" My Aunt Kristen was Mom's baby sister, their age gap a mere decade. It ran in our family, throwing the tree entirely out of whack.

"I can't wait to be finished," Maddie declared with a sigh. "Like, I already know where I'm going to school next year... everything's in place. The rest of senior year is just for show."

Had I ever felt that way? It was so long ago. "Do yourself a favor and appreciate the time you have left," I advised while the rest of the table nodded sagely. "You're going to look back and wish you hadn't been so determined for it to pass so quickly."

"Oh, because your life has been so miserable and unlucky since you left high school?" she challenged. She might have been the only girl in the world who could get away with smirking at me the way she did, lifting an eyebrow in a way that told me I was in for trouble. "I mean, you're only sitting here in your restaurant where thousands and thousands of people eat every year. You make, like, zillions of dollars."

"That's tacky," Mom admonished, shaking her head. "Besides, it's not zillions."

"How do you know?" I countered with a grin.

"You know what I mean," Maddie insisted, raising her voice to be heard over our soft laughter. "I'm just saying. Maybe don't lecture me when you've got a lot of good stuff going on in your life right now. Maybe I can't wait to get older so I can have nice things for myself too." She popped an olive in her mouth, shrugging.

"Oh, see?" Dad teased, winking at me. "She just wants to be like her big brother. Isn't that flattering?"

"Next thing I know, you'll be asking me for a job," I murmured, trying my best to look disapprovingly. The truth was, I would have loved it if Maddie decided to join me and make this a real family business. She had the guts and the moxie to make her way in the world, no matter what she decided to do.

I leaned back in my chair, taking my time, eating almost painfully slowly in an attempt to drag out the entrée portion of our meal. Platters lined the center of the table. Tonight's offerings included lasagna, Nonna's meatballs that had simmered on a low flame for ten hours before serving, grilled eggplant, and garlic sautéed greens. That, plus calamari and lemon shrimp had rounded out the meal. As always, I was stuffed to bursting, though I couldn't pretend the usual feeling of satisfaction came into play this evening. Normally, I looked forward to an opportunity to connect with my family, though the guests sometimes rotated depending on who was available. For instance, my cousins would stop in whenever they were in town, but they were off living their own lives. Regardless, they knew the door was always open. That was one policy that would never change—family was always welcome.

Tonight, it was the staff I was more concerned with, but then that was no surprise, at least to me. After last night's minor blowup in front of the rest of the kitchen, I made myself a promise not to antagonize her tonight.

It was one thing to force my way through dinner with my friends, who were wise enough to leave me the hell alone when it was clear I wasn't in a good mood, but my family? They would make it their business to glean every last bit of information they could.

There was no delaying the inevitable, and it was clear my sister's excitement grew as staff came out to clear the platters from the table, signaling the approach of dessert.

"If it's anywhere near as good as that bread..." Dad said, "... I think we're in for a real treat."

"Some things don't change around here," I reminded him, raising my voice slightly to make sure everyone heard. "I'm not trying to reinvent the wheel. I have a good thing going, and nothing matters more to me than maintaining that. So I wouldn't expect anything new tonight."

From the way Maddie's mouth opened, it was obvious she was ready to argue until she sat upright in her chair, nudging Mom with her elbow. "There she is! Oh my God, she's coming this way."

Fuck. It was difficult enough to affect a professional attitude toward Claudia when she wasn't nearby. I was supposed to do it now, with her standing over my shoulder? I made a point of angling my body in my chair, pretending I felt much kinder toward her than I did.

"Claudia Granger, meet my family." My jaw ached from forcing a smile while introducing the people around the table, especially when Maddie giggled and insisted on taking a video. Children. They didn't have the first clue.

What was worse? Watching her charm my family or how the light caught her hair and turned it to spun gold? My parents' obvious admiration or her warm, brilliant smile? There was no peeling my gaze from her as she made her way around the table.

She saved Nonna for last, and the table went quiet. "I am so happy to meet you," Claudia murmured, taking one of my grandmother's hands in both of hers. "I understand it's your recipes that have been adapted for the restaurant. This is a real pleasure."

What pissed me off more than anything was how sincere she sounded. Mom's happy little sigh didn't help matters. Neither did the way Maddie practically swooned with one hand on her chest while she filmed with the other. It was all a big show, nothing more than that. Couldn't they see it? No, they hadn't witnessed my pastry chef playing the part of the humble, gracious pseudo-celebrity night after night.

Meaning I had no choice but to grit my teeth and smile through everything, knowing she couldn't be sincere.

Nonna certainly didn't, which struck me as strange. My grandmother was usually the sharpest person I knew, the best judge of character. "The pleasure is mine," she insisted with a gentle laugh, her faded blue eyes shining. "I want you to know I rooted for you all season long."

Claudia laughed warmly. "Thank you, but I'll tell you, I thought the show was stressful, but that was before I got here," she confided in a stage whisper, glancing my way with a comical grimace. "Out of the frying pan and into the fire."

"Oh, don't you worry about my Sebastian," Nonna told her while I silently glowered. "His bark is much worse than his bite."

"I can handle myself, Nonna," I reminded her in a gentle voice, though it was Claudia whose gaze I sought and held when her bright, blue eyes locked onto mine at last. "No need to speak for me like I'm not here."

"Nobody could ever make the mistake of forgetting you're here," Claudia assured me with a sickeningly sweet smile. "You are the owner, after all."

She would do well to remember that, smarting off in front of my family.

Claudia's jaw twitched, her gaze lingered a beat, and then she turned her attention back to my grandmother. "I'll keep your advice in mind, though I might get a rabies shot in advance, just to be on the safe side." They shared another laugh while I finished what was left of the merlot in my glass. Fast friends already. How nice.

Once she was finished kissing Nonna's ass, Claudia looked over the length of the table, pointedly avoiding my gaze this time. "So, I did something a little different tonight. A slight variation on a seasonal dessert recipe. I hope you don't mind, but I figured if there's anyone I would want to sample this, it would be all of you."

No. She fucking. Didn't.

"Oh, I can't wait!" Maddie barely stopped short of bouncing out of her chair. "A new Claudia Granger recipe just for us?"

"Not a new recipe," Claudia gently corrected while I questioned my hearing because this certainly wasn't unfolding the way it seemed.

"What is it, then?" I asked, forcing her to look at me again. "Because it sounds a lot like a new recipe if you altered it somehow."

"It's a riff," she replied with that sunny, photogenic smile that twisted my guts. "I'll let you see for yourselves."

She glanced toward the kitchen door and crooked a finger to signal two servers who emerged carrying trays laden with plated tarts. "I understand the apple tart is based upon your apple pie," Claudia explained to Nonna as the tarts were placed before us. "I've added a couple of elements. I hope you enjoy it. If you don't, that's totally fine. I promise you won't hurt my feelings," she added with a soft laugh.

"It smells amazing," Maddie gushed, picking up her spoon and digging in without hesitation. I waited along with the rest of the family, watching her insert the spoon into her mouth without asking what had been added to the dish. She was that trusting.

Her eyes closed, her body sagged, and I knew what was coming. "Oh my God. What did you do? It's heaven," she sighed. The words were barely out of her mouth before she went for a second bite, at which point everyone began tasting for themselves. I took my time, gauging their reactions first, watching as, one by one, they adopted an expression every cook looked for —complete bliss.

"Oh, it's wonderful!" Mom declared. "There's a sort of… nuttiness? I can't put my finger on it." Her question inspired me to take a bite of what I wished didn't taste so damn balanced and rich. Was it good news for the restaurant? Sure, but she went over my head to make it happen. The sweet fruit soured in my mouth at the thought.

"Browned butter," Claudia explained, clearly pleased with herself. "With some shredded gruyere cheese in the crust, the addition of pears along with the apples, and a bit of brûléed finishing sugar. Then, of course, homemade cinnamon ice cream."

"Browned butter." Nonna smiled up at her, and envy twisted itself around my heart like barbed wire, digging in, drawing blood. "Why did I never think of that? It's delicious," she announced, taking one of Claudia's hands and squeezing.

"You really think so?" Was that a tremor in her

voice? Was it authentic? "I can't tell you what an honor it is to hear you say that."

"I am honored you improved upon my recipe," Nonna insisted. It was a real love fest, in other words, while all I could do was barely hold myself to a simmer as my family lost their mind over a little cheese and butter. I was not a man accustomed to sitting back and accepting shit, yet there was no choice now. Not unless I wanted to come off as a complete asshole in front of people who mattered.

"Truly, adding a new touch to a beloved recipe is one of the things I love most about what I do." With one last look over the table and an obvious beat during which our eyes locked for longer than necessary, Claudia concluded, "I'm so glad you're all happy. And I look forward to seeing you all again."

"I can't wait to try anything you make," Maddie assured her, making everyone laugh except me. The most I could manage was a grimace that left my jaw aching. That ache persisted throughout my goodbyes with the family, who asked if they could come back next week. I mumbled a thin excuse about the restaurant being booked solid and the amount of work that would soon go into opening my new location. Neither was a lie, but neither was sincere.

The truth? I couldn't stomach the thought of sitting through another ass-kissing session.

Although I took my time with the hugs and whatnot, my anger hadn't cooled by the time I strode from the front vestibule, where I'd waved goodbye to my parents as they drove past, into the kitchen. Heads turned at my entrance. There was only one I was interested in.

It had to be instinct that held my mouth shut. The fire blazing in my gut urged me, pulled me through the room, and demanded satisfaction. Nobody got away with putting me on the spot.

A pair of blue eyes followed my every step, but I ignored Claudia's pointed stare in favor of retreating to my office. The closed door did nothing to make me forget she was out there, considering herself God's gift to bakers by browning some fucking butter.

It took inserting AirPods in my ears and digging into a pile of invoices for the new restaurant to get me through the following hours. The girl might not have known it, but the only reason she was alive right now was because I'd stepped back from being head chef, giving me the chance to retreat to a locked room rather than being face-to-face behind the line. I might have had no choice but to request she leave for the night. Loudly.

By the time I'd sorted the invoices and reviewed updated timelines for completion, my playlist had run its course. I slid one of the pods from my ear, listening for sounds beyond the closed door. The kitchen was mostly quiet an hour after service had ended. No doubt anyone who'd left before now thought twice about knocking to say goodnight.

Maybe they had, and I'd missed it. Either way, it was for the best.

If Claudia possessed half a brain, she would've made a quick exit for fear of my wrath. Sadly, she didn't have the sense—either that or she'd waited on purpose—determined to test my self-control.

Only she and Lucas were left, chatting quietly by the ovens. He took a backward step away from her, like a guilty man. Fresh fire bloomed in my chest before I could help it. "Anything wrong?" I asked him.

He shook his head, lifting a thick shoulder. The guy would have looked right at home at the front door of a busy club, standing a head taller than most of the customers, ready to toss troublemakers out on their asses. Right now, his tanned complexion went a little pale. "Nope. Have a good one." That didn't keep him from glancing toward Claudia one last time, then quickly exiting through the back door.

Leaving the two of us. I'd let her take the first shot to see what she thought she was working with before eviscerating her for going behind my back.

Her tongue darted over her lips before she ventured, "Your family seems very nice. Your nonna is lovely."

"They are," I grunted, remembering how they'd bonded by joking about me. My anger began to simmer, verging on a boil. "She is."

Her soft, sharp sigh revealed her frustration. "Just get it over with, okay? I know you've been waiting."

"You're lucky I've been waiting. I could've done this while the rest of the staff was present." The pressure in my chest spread, tightening my throat, putting my head in a vice. "Now that we're alone, I want you to tell me *where the fuck* you get off putting me on the spot."

She scoffed. "Because it's all about you. It wasn't about me wanting to—"

"Enough!" The volume of my voice made her shrink back, eyes bulging. "I don't want to hear it. You chose tonight to present that new... what did you call it? A riff? Because you knew you could get away with it in front of them."

"Did you bother tasting it?" she snapped, her volume reaching mine. I liked it, perversely enough, knowing she had fire in her. It added color to her cheeks and left her chest heaving with every quick breath. I didn't realize I was staring until my dick twitched, forcing me to get my shit together.

"I did, which you'd know if you weren't so busy basking in adulation."

"Oh! Forgive me!" She touched a hand to her chest, drawing my gaze again. Dammit. "Was I soaking in the appreciation and praise of people whose opinion matters? I can see now why you're so bitter. You're dead set on hating me and everything I do."

That wasn't true. Was it? "Do not put words in my mouth," I warned, taking a step closer the way a moth floated close to a flame that might kill it. There was no resisting the pull she had on me and how it intensified when things heated up between us.

She instantly pulled back, her chest rising and falling with each shallow breath as I stood close. "Oh, please," she scoffed. "A child could see straight through you. Quit the gaslighting."

I was going to fire her. There was no other way around it. No way I could coexist with this woman without blood being shed. "I expressly requested—"

"You requested nothing. You ordered," she spat. "You bullied. You did *not* request. And I am sorry..." she continued, biting off her words through clenched teeth, "... but I will not stifle myself creatively because you're too afraid to take a few chances in this kitchen. You wonder why your brand is on the decline? Why don't you take a look at how stale and repetitive your menu is?"

With a bitter laugh, I asked, "You haven't been here a full week, and I'm supposed to take your opinion seriously?"

"I know what I'm talking about."

"Oh right." I snapped my fingers, chuckling. "I forgot. You're an expert. Somebody put you on TV, and you know everything there is about building a brand and maintaining it for years."

Her face darkened, and her eyes blazed like the fire crisping my insides. "You know something? If someone was trying to sabotage you, I can understand why."

Motherfucker. I sucked in a breath, reeling inside

but unwilling to reveal it. She knew how to hit below the belt. There was crossing the line, and there was dancing her way over it. The girl had full-on waltzed.

She knew it, too, falling back a step, even gasping softly like she couldn't believe herself. "I'm... I shouldn't—"

Slicing my hand through the air, I cut her off. "I'm not interested in hearing whatever it is you're trying to say. You've already said more than enough." I struggled to contain myself as it was, fighting against revealing how deeply those words sliced through my core.

Her throat worked. "I'm sorry," she whispered. "For what I said. Not for the tart, though."

The stubborn little thing. I didn't know whether to laugh or scream as she stood at her full height, which wasn't saying much, and glared up at me in defiance. She had heart, grit, and I would have appreciated both in anyone but her.

Her perfume hit me before I even realized I'd been leaning in, and I had to shake myself back to reality. "Do us both a favor and get out of my sight," I muttered because there was no winning this fight. No firing her without coming off like a whiny bitch. No stopping her from experimenting since she knew she had me by the balls now. My family loved her almost as much as they loved her baking.

It was a good thing she did as I asked for once.

I might have done something I couldn't undo.

6

CLAUDIA

The pretty, stylish girl seated across from me leaned in a little like we were about to share secrets. Her eyes gleamed almost as brightly as her smile when she asked, "Really, what is it like to work with Sebastian Kennedy?"

Talk about a loaded question, but then the thirty minutes we'd spent together so far had been filled to bursting with innuendo and attempts at getting me to badmouth my fellow competitors. Eight months after the competition's end, people were still stuck on whether I kept in touch with anyone or if things were ever as strained as they appeared on camera—more drama manufactured by the producers. There wasn't much a clever editor couldn't pull off.

Now, the conversation was turning from the generalities of adjusting to so-called normal life to the specifics of working with my braindead boss. The angel and devil on my shoulders fought for dominance, both filling my head with what I should say. Things like...

"There's a reason Sebastian Kennedy has made it as far as he has. It's an honor and a privilege to share a kitchen with him and learn all he has to teach. He is also distractingly hot."

"Sebastian Kennedy is a self-important, self-righteous, talentless pain in the ass. Oh, and he's gorgeous too."

It's funny how they both wanted me to comment on how distractingly attractive he was.

Boy, would it feel good to unburden myself and share exactly what I'd been through the past couple of weeks. I'd bitten my tongue so many times it was a miracle the thing was still attached and functional. I had come to crave the peace of him being away from the restaurant, busy with plans for his upcoming opening. We were still two months away, but there were meetings, phone calls, and plans to be approved. I couldn't wait for the time when he would have to split the hours between one location and the other. I flat-out looked forward to it and hoped he spent the bulk of his time over there on the other end of the Strip, far away from me.

But sharing something like that wouldn't make for good press, and good press was what I was looking to drum up. If not for his sake, definitely for mine. "It has been a real learning experience," I explained, using the words I'd practiced countless times in preparation for this interview with a local food writer. "This is my first time working in a large, thriving kitchen like the one Sebastian runs at Home. I love the pace, I love the energy, and the people are fantastic."

I knew when her eyes narrowed for a fraction of a second that I was cooked. "But what about Sebastian himself?"

"What about him?" I asked with a soft laugh, which I hoped wouldn't betray my nerves. Was this for real? I was doing my best to get out of this without insulting anyone, but she wanted her 'gotcha' moment. I seriously regretted ever agreeing to this piece, but it was all about squeezing every last drop out of my short-lived fame.

"He's notoriously inflexible." She offered a tiny wince like she felt sorry for me. "What does that mean for an up-and-coming chef who wants to make a name for herself? Isn't it frustrating being held back?"

What had started as suspicion was beginning to turn into certainty. Folding my hands in my lap, I asked, "Why does it seem like you're trying to corner me into saying something I don't intend to say? I didn't come here to have words inserted into my mouth," I reminded her as gently as I could while inside, I was beginning to seethe. "With due respect, I would prefer sticking to the questions your editor forwarded to me before our meeting."

"Oh, I'm sorry." Somebody needed to tell the girl that when she said she was sorry, she should at least try to look or sound that way. "I didn't mean to offend you. You know how it is... people have certain expectations. I'm sure you've seen a lot of that in the follow-up from your success."

I had seen a lot of things in the follow-up from my success. For instance, how fleeting it could be. How fickle people were. How, in a world where reality competitions were being filmed and produced all the time, there was no longevity. There would always be somebody new around the corner, waiting to claim their few minutes of fame.

There was no such thing as resting. Breathing. I'd zigzagged across the country in the weeks after my victory, capitalizing on the freshness of my success. But by the time the offers had dried up, once my name no longer stopped people in their tracks and I wasn't being mentioned on morning talk shows anymore, it was clear my time had passed. I couldn't even get my own show, the way my agent was so sure I would in the aftermath. Not that I wanted my own show—that had never been on the horizon for me. But it went to show how easy it was for the public to turn away and forget.

I was beyond relieved when the interview ended, and I was free to leave the café. Initially, I had planned on going home to catch up on some sleep afterward. I only got one day off a week, and sleep had sort of fallen pretty far down my priorities. I was too wired for sleep, though, and not only due to the iced latte I drank during the interview. It was so obvious that the so-called reporter was trying to trick me into saying something inflammatory.

And while Sebastian Kennedy irked me in just about every conceivable way, I wasn't trying to put him on blast in front of all of Las Vegas and anyone else who happened to read that article. All I needed was for word to spread that I enjoyed biting the hand that fed me.

Wouldn't it have been nice, though? Telling her exactly what I thought? The idea brought a grim smile, which was the only kind of smile I could muster upon entering my almost pitifully small apartment. It was a hole in the wall, but all I could afford at the moment with my savings dwindling. Yes, my award came with a hefty cash prize, but along with that came hefty taxes, not to mention the money that went to my agent each time she booked me an appearance on one television show or another. Las Vegas wasn't exactly known for its low cost of living, either.

Yet another reason to despise Brandon for what he did to me and for hating Shelby, thanks to her part in the betrayal. Somebody who was supposed to be a friend, a supporter, a collaborator once we started working together. To think, they had the nerve to act like it was an accident. Like he had laid down in my bed, butt naked, and she had accidentally fallen on his dick. *Whoopsie.*

They had worked together to destroy my life, crush my spirit, and force me to drive all the way out here to the desert where Sebastian Kennedy could finish the job.

The thought of him made me ball up my sundress once I'd pulled it off, then throw it across the room in a pitiful attempt to vent my anger. The prick went out of his way to glare coldly at me whenever our paths crossed. He wouldn't come out and call me a bitch or threaten my job. It was much more fun for him to glower at me and keep me guessing. I knew when he told me to leave the kitchen the night of his family dinner that the war was by no means over. He had retreated, but only briefly to regroup.

Once I was dressed in my typical tee and shorts, I considered what to do with the rest of the day. Rather than flop down on the double bed in the living room, which also served as my bedroom, I turned to the tiny kitchen area. Really, it was nothing more than a corner of the single room that served as my home, aside from a bathroom too small to fit more than one person at a time unless one of them was in the tub.

I could spend the day fighting for any tiny bit of counter space here, or I could go to the restaurant and work on a few new recipes while it was closed as usual on a Monday. No matter what the so-called great Sebastian wanted to believe, he needed new dishes for the new restaurant. He probably only thought he understood what his diners wanted, like he thought the concept of pairing bread with a complimentary dipping oil was too avant-garde to be believed.

As usual, a woman would have to convince a man of what was best for him, but I'd have to take the long route around his ego. And his was bigger than most.

Thinking about the size of his hands, I had to wonder if certain other parts of him were also big. *Stop it!* As if I needed to blur the line of professionalism any worse than we already had.

The short drive passed quickly, my thoughts on what I wanted to do once I reached the kitchen. I'd been toying with the idea of a deconstructed cobbler lately, or maybe a play on tiramisu. Something that wouldn't deviate too far from Sebastian's original concept. I could fill dessert cups with the mascarpone mixture, add ladyfingers on top, maybe pour an espresso and amaretto syrup over the top...

Few things could slow me down on my way through the locked door behind the restaurant's kitchen, but a call from my best friend was one of them. I paused beside a stack of empty milk crates and answered, "Hadley, my love," I sighed, searching for the right key on the heavy ring I carried.

"Claudia, my love," she chirped. Her cheerful voice reminded me of everything I'd left behind by fleeing the East Coast. "How did your interview go?"

"Ugh." I settled for leaving it there while unlocking the back door, deactivating the alarm, and flipping on the lights. Nothing compares to a sparkling, quiet kitchen. It felt as calming as stepping into a spa.

"I'm sorry. But hey, it's all part of being a star." Her

comically breathless voice pulled a laugh out of me even when I was determined to be annoyed.

"All she wanted to talk about was working with you-know-who." I was afraid to say his name. What if I summoned him somehow? Like a demon or something.

She knew all about him thanks to our many conversations, which was why she surprised me by countering, "Come on. Don't tell me it's not at least a little bit fun working with somebody like him."

"There are millions of hot men in the world, Hadley," I muttered, shaking my head as I pulled out ingredients for ladyfingers. Maybe I'd add cocoa powder to them, eliminate the amaretto factor…

"Sure, but are they all rich? Famous? Right in front of you all the time?" When I only groaned, she kept going. "All I can do is imagine you two in close quarters, sweating it out. There's a million customers waiting for their food, and you have to work together to keep them all happy. Then all of a sudden, your eyes meet as your hands brush, and you realize what a great team you make."

That sounded nice. I sort of hated how nice it sounded. "If only it were that easy," I murmured, distracted by the mental image of Sebastian staring into my eyes, realizing what a good team we made. He was gorgeous—stormy gray eyes and a jawline I both wanted and wanted to punch. I was only human.

"So that's what you want to happen?" Hadley teased.

Whoa. Time to tune back into the conversation. "No, but it would be nice if there weren't so much antagonism between us all the time," I admitted while separating eggs, adding the whites to a mixing bowl. I could use the yolks in the filling...

"Ooh, tension," she whispered, giggling.

"Not the kind you're thinking about," I insisted.

"Oh, come on." She groaned like I had truly broken her heart. "Don't destroy my fantasies here. You mean to tell me it's not like that at all?"

Everything I wanted to unload on that interviewer came rushing to the surface. I could only hold back for so long, and my friendship with Hadley was my safe place—the only safe place left in my life. "He's ignorant. He's arrogant. And he is so ridiculously afraid of change, making it impossible for me to function. I can't do anything new, I swear. Everything has to stay exactly the same. Anybody could do this job."

One silent beat after another passed before she deadpanned, "Explain to me what the problem is because I'm not getting it."

"I'm starting to think you're deliberately not getting it."

"I'm not interested in him that way," I insisted, raising my voice over her soft disagreement and the whirring of the mixer as I beat the egg whites. "I was really, really hoping this position would lead to bigger things. How can it possibly lead to bigger things if all he wants me to do is recreate the same tired recipes week in and week out? They're not even recipes I developed, for God's sake," I added with a bitter laugh, turning toward the prep table to measure flour. "And when I try to make a small change, he acts like I squatted on the prep table and pissed all over everything." I slapped a hand against the prep table for emphasis, sending bits of flour flying. It wouldn't be the first time I'd made a mess out of myself.

"I'm sorry. I shouldn't joke like that," she admitted, sounding regretful now that I had unloaded on her. "What can we do about this?" One thing I loved about her was the way she could turn things around.

"We can't do anything. Only I can, and I don't know what." With a sigh, I added, "You know I love you for saying it that way. "

"Hey. There's never been anything we haven't been able to do together once we combine our ridiculous intelligence and creativity." She had never lacked confidence.

"I wish I had been half as intelligent as you back when you were telling me to kick Brandon to the curb." No amount of gently folding flour into the egg whites could calm the bitterness that always rose to the surface when his stupid face came to mind—that little-boy smile, the innocence he so easily faked.

"Yeah, you really don't know how challenging it was not to smack you upside the head sometimes." She paused, then added, "I saw him yesterday. He asked me about you."

"He didn't have the balls," I growled.

"You're surprised at his ballsiness after all this?" she asked while I muttered ten different kinds of ugliness under my breath. "He knew I would tell you, which is why he did it. And here I am, playing into his hand."

There was one question that rang out in the forefront of my mind right away. "How did he look?"

Her low, wicked laughter answered the question before she said a word. "Like hell."

"You're just saying that." Of course, I had to add, "Tell me more."

She giggled before it burst out of her. "Oh my God, I've been dying to tell you. Were you the only person in that relationship who knew how to use an iron? Because his clothes were all wrinkled, he needs a haircut, and I'm pretty sure he misplaced his razor because he was rocking at least four days of stubble."

"You're not just playing it up to make me feel better?" I asked while carefully filling a piping bag.

"Obviously, if I were playing it up to make you feel better, I would've told you his dick fell off."

My laughter filled the room. "How would you know unless you saw for yourself?"

"Ew. I'm not trying to see that."

Laughing felt good. It loosened the tightness in my chest. "What I wouldn't give to go to brunch and sit with you and a bottomless mimosa," I said with a sigh.

"Well, why can't we?"

Piping onto parchment paper, I snorted. "There's those pesky thousands of miles between us."

"So? I'll come to you." I snorted again, and she replied, "I'm serious. I've got tons of miles saved up and tons of vacation time too. I'll come out to see you… make sure you're taking care of yourself."

I didn't get the chance to reply when a sharp question rang out, making me jump. "What the fuck are you doing here?"

The ladyfinger I was piping turned into a zigzag while my head snapped up to find Sebastian standing with his arms folded, staring daggers at me. The athletic clothes he wore told me he was in the middle of a workout when something brought him here.

"I get a text telling me somebody disarmed the alarm on the one day a week we're closed, and I find you fucking around in the kitchen," he growled. Shit. I hadn't thought about that.

"Oh my God," Hadley whispered in my ear. "Is that him? He sounds hot."

Not what I needed to hear. "Gotta go," I murmured, ending the call before she could beg me to kiss him.

"What are you doing?" he demanded, staring at the parchment where, until he'd come in, I'd been piping perfect ladyfingers.

"Building a space shuttle. Isn't it obvious?" Blowing

a strand of hair out of my eyes, I said, "Working on an idea."

"You and your ideas are going to give me a fucking heart attack." He threw his hands into the air. "I'm on my way to meet with my trainer, and the next thing I know, I'm pulling a U-turn to haul ass over here."

"Sorry about that." I couldn't say I was sorry to see him, even if that wasn't my goal and showing up here. I had never seen him looking this casual. The sight of his thick calves and defined forearms revealed by his shorts and T-shirt did strange, unexpected things to my insides.

It was a good thing he decided to be a prick since it reminded me who I was dealing with. "This kitchen isn't your testing ground, and I'm not wasting money on ingredients for you to fuck around with."

"No, you would rather spend money on ingredients baked into desserts fewer and fewer people order all the time," I fired back before I could help it.

Well, it had to come out eventually.

"I'm sorry to put it that way," I babbled while he sputtered, fighting to find something to say. "But you might as well hear it now before you open the new location. You need to change things up a little. You're already losing money when it comes to that part of the menu."

"Anything else you would like to tell me about how to run my business?" With his hands on his hips, he looked me up and down, his steely eyes narrowed. “You seem to be such an expert.”

We had a problem much bigger than the warmth growing low in my belly. When he moved just right, his broad chest was more clearly revealed beneath his cotton shirt, and it kept drawing my attention. That was an issue, for sure.

The real problem was knowing he would never pay attention to anything I had to say now, in this mood. I could defend myself, I could present numbers, and he wouldn’t give a damn. That was why I blurted out the last thing I had intended to share. “I don’t believe in waste. Wasting food is something I make sure never to do if I can help it. I spent too long never knowing where the next meal would come from to take anything for granted now.”

It wasn’t what I intended to do, but it was the perfect thing to say. I watched while much of his anger drained away.

“I’m sorry to hear that,” he eventually grunted.

“It’s not something I talk about.” I stared down at the row of ladyfingers. They were losing volume, thanks to the fact that I still stood here without putting them in the oven. “With that in mind, I’m going to bake these because I’ve already prepared them. Just... trust me for once. I haven’t steered you wrong yet.”

He didn’t say anything at first, settling for a jerk of his chin. I transferred the parchment to a baking sheet, then slid it carefully into the preheated oven and set the timer. Why did it always have to feel like I was at war with this man?

"I wasn't raised with money, you know." His sudden admission startled me, though I did my best not to show it as I turned back toward him. He was leaning against the prep table now, arms folded, ankles crossed. "Nonna... she grew up very poor. To tell you the truth, my favorite dishes of hers are the ones she pulled together in the early days of her marriage before my grandfather's restaurant took off."

"I didn't realize your grandfather had a restaurant."

"Yeah, and it killed him by the time he turned forty-five." There was a bitter twist to his mouth. "There's a reason I decided to step down as head chef. The job killed him before his time, and I didn't want the same to happen to me."

He looked at the floor, blowing out a breath through pursed lips. "When I told my family I wanted to open a restaurant and carry on his legacy, you don't know the sort of pushback I got. I thought they'd be happy. Instead, I was reminded twenty different times in twenty different ways how the restaurant business had killed my grandfather. How it left Mom and her brother without a father, how it meant Nonna having to work night and day to make ends meet. There's a reason I have them over for dinner so frequently," he added with a glance my way. "So they can check up on me, make sure I'm not working myself to death. It's not much of a sacrifice, especially considering all the support they've given me."

Now I understood maybe much more than he intended to reveal. There I was, giving him shit for never wanting to deviate from his menu. What could it have done to him, hearing all the terrible stuff about how his grandfather died young? The tried-and-true meant safety.

But there was nothing safe about this business.

He had to know that.

Clearing his throat, he straightened up, looking around. "So long as you promise not to wreck the place, go ahead. Maybe give me a heads-up next time before you walk in here on a day we're closed."

"Only if you promise not to give me shit for it."

He rolled his eyes but paired it with a grin. "Can you take a victory for once without asking for better terms?"

"I don't know. I've never tried," I retorted.

"Oh? Did you ask for different terms when you won your big competition?"

This again. "Enough with the fucking competition!" I must have lost my mind for a moment because the next thing I knew, I was taking a small handful of flour off the prep table and flinging it at him. "I swear to God, you mention it again, I'll lock you in the walk-in!"

Flour spattered his black shorts and bare calves. "What the fuck?" he asked, but there was laughter in his voice. "What, are you so short that was the best you could do?"

So that was how he wanted to play. "Fine." This time, I very deliberately flung another handful in his face. "How's that?"

"An excuse to do this." It was his turn, and he made me pay, flinging a fistful of it on me from above. I shook my head, causing a cloud of dust to form around me.

"It's an improvement," he decided. I could imagine him teasing his sister this way, and a flash of longing swept through me. If he could always be this nice, we'd get along much better. We might become more of a partnership than adversaries.

All at once, the situation shifted. It was the change in his gaze, the light in his eyes and how it darkened, and how serious he suddenly looked and moved in all at once, his hands outstretched like he was about to touch me. My heart leaped, and my body went hot from head to toe because, yes, I wanted that. I didn't know how much I wanted it until this very moment, with desire swelling in my core and making it seem like a great idea to get carried away. To forget being smart in favor of seeing what kind of kisser he was.

The moment passed, and I remembered my career, dreams, and bruised heart. That was why I scurried backward and hit the table. When he touched me, it was to keep me from falling, his steadying hands on my waist. Even that was almost too much, sending heat racing through me again. He was so close.

"Thanks," I mumbled, pivoting away from him to avoid us making a mistake. My heart sank, yes, especially when he released me, and the current flowing from his body into mine was cut off. It was enough of a struggle to keep from letting myself think of him this way without his touch making the job ten times harder.

He cleared his throat, "Right." He let go, stepped back, and turned away like the whole thing never happened. "I, uh... I'm leaving. Don't forget to set the alarm when you go."

"Mm-hmm." I didn't trust myself to speak without tripping over my tongue.

What the hell was that?

And why the hell did I want it so badly?

7

SEBASTIAN

"As you can see, gentlemen, things are coming along well." Turning my back on the trio of investors who scheduled this meeting, I gazed out over the structure that would soon be christened as my second restaurant. There was still a hell of a lot to be done, but it had been a joy so far to drive by every day and note the differences as time went on. The original structure had been completely torn down once it was clear rebuilding would be cheaper than remodeling, bringing practically ancient code and standards up to date.

Felix had joined me for this, and I had to wonder if it wasn't his way of checking up on me. For the most part, he had stayed quiet after essentially strongarming me into hiring Claudia, and he had yet to bring her up while touring this impromptu tour of our new facility. After we'd shown the men around inside, I brought them out to admire the façade, including what would be a beautiful outdoor dining area placed beneath a pergola where grape vines would grow and wind around the wooden slats overhead. I could imagine the area on comfortable, cool nights filled with twinkling lights and the warmth of flickering candles lining long tables. A sense of family, community, coming together. It was all I wanted, my ultimate goal at all times.

Unfortunately, the investors needed to be satisfied as well. I was thankful to see nothing but smiles as I described the vision while Felix unrolled artist renderings for them to study. I could release a deep breath and, along with it, some of my anxiety. I worked like hell to conceal it, but it was still there, bubbling under the surface.

"How are things with your newest hire?" Peter Clearfield, one of my original and most trusted investors, turned to me wearing a knowing grin. "I've heard she's a real ball buster."

"Sure, but it takes a ball buster to get shit done," added Maxwell Andrews, sounding like the hard-bitten old man he was. I needed fresh blood, young investors, but for the time being was surrounded by the old boys' club. They had their place, just like ball-busters did, but at the moment, my patience was a bit thin. I couldn't bring myself to feign good humor while the three of them chuckled knowingly, eyeing me up like they were waiting for some juicy bit of gossip to drop from my lips. There were times they were no better than chattering old women.

"Just look at the numbers from these last few weeks." As usual, Felix brought things around to dollars and cents, which, in the end, was all any of them had any right to ask about. The condition of their investment, whether they would earn healthy returns. "Revenue has effectively doubled. Not that we were doing that poorly in the first place, but customers are staying longer, ordering more food, bringing friends. The buzz is terrific, and the puff pieces scheduled for publishing in the local papers and food blogs are only going to boost the numbers further."

"I hate to say it, Sebastian, but we were right." Something told me Nicholas Davis didn't hate it one damn bit. No more than I would in his place if I had given him my money to invest in a business. At least he didn't make a big deal of rubbing my nose in it.

"You know I always trust you gentlemen to steer me in the right direction." If this didn't end soon, their asses would end up chafed from all the kissing I was doing, to say nothing of my self-respect. Thankfully, they were busy men, taking their leave with promises to catch up in the coming weeks. I couldn't pretend there was anything but relief in watching them go, the three of them driving away in cars much too young and flashy for anyone of their advanced ages.

The last tires had barely rolled from what would be

the parking lot when Felix turned to me. "There's a problem."

I couldn't have a single minute of self-satisfaction without cold reality being thrown in my face. "What the hell is wrong now?" Sweat began prickling under my collar, so I popped the top button and loosened my tie. Rather than stand out in the open under a blazing sun, I followed Felix inside the building. I had suggested this Saturday morning for our meeting since there was no work scheduled to be done today. We had the place to ourselves.

Good thing, too, because he had the sort of news I needed to hear in private. "We've had some issues with permits," Felix informed me, removing his glasses to wipe them with his striped tie. "I got a call from my guy at the union, and he said there's a lot of double-talk going on. One person says one thing, another says something completely different, but the message is the same... we're being held up on this. We can't move forward with work until the permit situation is cleared up."

"What the fuck?" My shouted question echoed off the walls and floors. The sweet smell of sawdust in my nose paired well with the bitterness in my throat. "Why the hell was I not informed of this?"

"I got the call late last night," he explained, though his explanations weren't worth much at the moment.

"Who the hell is responsible for this? Permits. I thought all the permits were lined up and taken care of by now, or else we never could've gotten this off the ground in the first place." I was wasting my breath, taking my anger and frustration out on someone who could do nothing about it.

"I hear you," he insisted, looking and sounding pained. Now I noticed his gray pallor, the dark circles under his eyes. He'd done his best to look bright and chipper for the sake of the investors, but now was a different story. "And I'm working to get to the bottom of it. But I wanted to let you know in case you get word that work doesn't pick back up Monday morning."

"Well, thanks for keeping me in the loop," I growled, ignoring his exasperated sigh in favor of pulling out my phone. "I need to get to the restaurant. I'm going to call a friend of mine and see if there's anything he can do."

"Keep me posted on anything you hear," he urged, following me out, waiting while I locked up. *Motherfucker.* Just when I thought all of that backstabbing, shady bullshit was over. As if I needed something else to be concerned about. One more hurdle, one more roadblock.

I waited until Grayson picked up the call, then connected him to the car's Bluetooth, and pulled out from the lot. "I've got a problem," I told him, the words coming out flat. "I was thinking you might be just the person to help me with it."

His knowing laughter filled the Lamborghini's interior. "Depends upon the kind of problem we're talking about. You know, I'm going to start charging for my services."

He had to be referring to the work he and his team of freelance security guards had performed a few months back when Vaughn's wife, Nova, was in hiding from her criminal father and his team of henchmen. The fact was, none of us asked for many details when it came to Grayson's work. There were some things we didn't need to know about. He seemed to prefer it that way.

All the same, it was helpful knowing he had connections none of us could boast. "Felix just told me about some permit issues with the labor union, and it looks like there's been a stop put on all construction work at the new location. This is completely out of the clear blue since everything was running smoothly until now."

"Son of a bitch," he grumbled, and it was a gratifying sound. Knowing I wasn't the only one baffled and angered by these constant setbacks.

"Would you happen to know anyone who could do a little digging for me?" I cringed at the question since I hated calling in a favor like this, especially knowing he hated being put on the spot as much as I did. But we went back long enough that I felt I could ask. "I need to know who is behind this shit, once and for all."

"Thank fuck," he muttered. "I've been waiting for you to ask. It took you long enough."

I barked out a laugh. "Seriously?" I asked, stopping

at a red light and watching handfuls of tourists crossing in both directions, completely oblivious, gazing up at the signs and structures that weren't half as impressive during the day as they were at night.

"I was going to look into it for you, but I thought you might take it the wrong way. Like it would be the same as accusing you of not being able to handle your shit."

The thing was, I probably would have taken it that way. Now, I could only be grateful. "Thanks, man. You know how much this means. I owe you one."

"Please," he muttered with a chuckle. "Let's not start keeping track now."

It was good to laugh with a friend, though my jovial mood did not last the time it took to reach the rear entrance of Home. The number of cars parked in a long row told me the kitchen would be full, as it needed to be. Unless we were able to resolve this permit issue soon, I would need all the good news I could gather to keep the investors happy. Eventually, they were bound to find out things had slowed down.

I expected to be bombarded by the musical clang of pots, pans, spoons, and spatulas. Upon stepping into the kitchen through the back door, I found an almost eerie quiet punctuated by a single voice. "When asked to comment on the experience of working with a seasoned pro with a winning track record, Granger was surprisingly tight-lipped."

Lucas. It sounded like he was reading aloud. The

beating of my heart was a bass drum in my ears as I approached slowly, silently, rounding the corner where my office sat and finding the kitchen crew gathered around him. He stood in the center of the group and read aloud from what looked like a slim magazine. The only person missing was Claudia. She said something about a friend of hers coming to town today, something I had dismissed at the time while preparing for the investor meet-up this morning.

The mention of her name popped the swollen balloon of tension in my skull and flooded me with red-hot resentment. "I'm sorry. Are we off today?" I barked, watching everyone jump and cringe. "What the hell is going on around here?"

It was like magic, the effect the sound of my voice had on the people in my kitchen. They instantly found something better to do than stand around bullshitting like they'd been when they didn't realize I was here.

I turned to Lucas, who should know better. "Well? Did I miss the memo? I realize it's a weekend for some people but not for us."

"Sorry, boss. Somebody came by with an advance copy of tomorrow's article." Before I could ask what the hell he meant, he handed over an "Arts and Leisure" insert from the local paper. It bore Sunday's date. "An interview Claudia gave with the food writer over at the paper."

He didn't need to tell me once I saw the title of the article. *Can* America's Best Baker *Shake Up Home's Life?*

Goddammit. The paper crinkled in my hand once my fist began to tighten.

America's Best Baker *is cagey when asked for details about Sebastian Kennedy, long heralded as the genius behind Home's beloved if slightly repetitive offerings. Then again, isn't half the charm of going to Home knowing exactly what to expect? When viewed through that lens, it's clear Mr. Kennedy gives his customers what they want.*

Which is why it seems so out of character for him to bring a fresh, new face into his familiar and beloved establishment. With the opening of a second location in the coming months, a development long anticipated by critics and diners alike, one couldn't be blamed for wondering if he wants to offer something new.

However, one has to wonder how many risks he's willing to take when tried and true has worked for so long.

"Sebastian knows what he wants." Claudia Granger's ready smile is a familiar one to any fan. She approaches our sit-down with the same cheerfulness and professionalism she displayed through twelve weeks of grueling hell, pitted against bakers from around the world. "It's a pleasure to work with someone who possesses such a strong, almost rigid vision. There's no room for guessing, which means the focus can be left squarely on execution. It's a gift, really."

I get to the end of the first page and then realize the kitchen went silent. My head snapped up from the article—that was their cue to get moving, and they did, wasting no time in their prep work. Familiar aromas came back to me—onions, tomatoes, beef. Several prep cooks worked at rolling pasta sheets through a hand-cranked machine while another piped herbed ricotta, creating tortellini for tonight's soup.

But always, they glanced my way from the corners of their eyes, ever aware of my presence.

Rather than put on a public show a minute longer, I retreated to my office, closed the door, tossed the magazine onto my desk, and dropped into my chair. I needed this like I needed a hole in the head. It wasn't enough that one of my best friends was now using his connections to find out for sure whether or not I was being sabotaged, I needed the sabotage to come from my own kitchen?

I could see her in my mind's eye. The wide, charming smile of hers that seemed to fool everyone else into believing she was genuine. So smug, sure of herself, affecting that *aw-shucks* persona everyone fell for.

I closed my eyes, practiced breathing slowly, inhaling through my nose and exhaling through pursed lips. There was no calming myself in a moment like this. I didn't have a chance. Who *the fuck* did she think she was?

It was torture, and I knew it, but I couldn't stay away. I had to know what else she said, meaning I opened my eyes and picked up the article, flipping the page in a twisted example of masochism.

When asked about working with someone like Sebastian Kennedy, specifically, the chef is noncommittal at best.

"I love the fast pace of the kitchen, and the people are phenomenal," she tells me before requesting I stick to the list of prepared questions forwarded to her by our editor. She offers nothing when asked about new pastries the public can look forward to, only hinting at subtle changes. "Why fix what isn't broken?" she points out with a strained smile, then changes the subject.

It looks like Sebastian isn't the only kitchen member afraid to riff and be spontaneous, though the jury is out on whether that's due to his influence or not.

Crumpling the pages, I threw them across the room. A room that had gone red, a room now filled with my heavy breathing.

If anything, I should have been glad for this reminder of what this was all about and why she had come here in the first place. Not to intrigue me, not to arouse me, though she had done both, especially in the days since that near kiss earlier this week. I'd made it a point to steer clear of her since then, and she seemed to do the same. It had been a mistake, nothing more, and it hadn't affected our working relationship. If anything, it meant giving her the space she craved since every time our eyes met, I couldn't help but recall how hypnotic hers were in those final moments before I made the mistake of touching her.

It was too easy, letting my guard down, letting her get closer. We related too well to each other when it came to our work and passions. I couldn't remember the last time a woman had interested me that way, if ever.

She had already given this interview at that point, hadn't she? She fucking knew what that goddamn excuse for a reporter was going to say, and she hadn't bothered giving me a heads-up. The snake in the grass. The backstabber.

The woman whose voice now rang out cheerfully in the kitchen. "Hi, hi," Claudia called out, her voice getting louder as she drew closer to my door. "I just stopped in to make sure things are looking good before picking up my friend at the airport."

She had no idea what she had walked into, but I was ready to show her. This was my reward for letting my guard down, for letting her know me a little better. She had taken a shit all over my trust. Grabbing for the ruined magazine, I then flung the door open.

"Granger." My voice echoed in the kitchen once I stepped from my office, making her spin in place with her mouth hanging open and her eyes bulging. Didn't she look like a breath of fresh air in a flowered sundress, her hair loose around her shoulders? Softer than she normally appeared at work, bringing to mind the pair of cutoffs she'd worn during our surprise encounter earlier in the week.

"Kennedy?" she murmured before releasing a soft, disbelieving laugh. "What did I do wrong this time?"

"You might think you're being funny, but I'm not laughing." Thrusting the crumpled article her way, I explained, "You got what you wanted. It wasn't enough to go behind my back in the kitchen. You had to undermine me in the press too."

She took it from me, smoothing it out somewhat as her eyes darted back and forth across the surface. "Wait a second. No, hold on." With a groan, she dropped her arms to the sides, shaking her head. "I went out of my way—"

"To make me look like an asshole!" I barked. "Making me out to be some castrated little bitch who's strangling your precious creativity. Congratulations. You made sure the whole world knows what a piece of shit you think I am."

Her face went red before she shouted back, "She intended to make you look like the bad guy before I ever sat down with her!" I had to be imagining this, the way she spoke to me in front of the rest of my employees. "If there's any fault here, it's with me for not warning you. I am sorry for that... it slipped my mind."

"Oh, right. How convenient." As if she had ever intended to do that.

"It's the goddamn truth!"

"You know what, I don't care about your idea of the truth. Get the hell out of here, pick up your friend, and don't forget to tell her what a bastard I am when you do. Maybe she'll believe your half-assed bullshit because I don't."

Retreating to my office, I slammed the door, but the sound did nothing to cool my boiling rage. She expected me to believe she'd forgotten to warn me about a potential hit piece, and I was supposed to believe it had nothing to do with her feeling put off by my attempted kiss?

The masochist in me reared its ugly head again, this time convincing me to peer through the closed blinds separating me from the kitchen. I rarely opened them since my time in this room was meant to be private. Nobody wanted the boss watching them through a window all day, either.

She was still there, reading the article she'd spread out on the prep table she normally used. Her palms rested on the stainless-steel surface, her head hanging low while she reread the text. Her shoulders rose and fell in a quick, shallow rhythm that expressed her barely contained emotion.

Lucas joined her, sliding up close to where she stood. I watched, holding my breath, while he ran a hand in slow circles over her back and murmured something probably intended to comfort her.

She didn't stop him.

There was something almost possessive in the gesture, not to mention the way he hovered over her. Her protector, her guardian angel.

He had a fucking thing for her.

The realization ignited something fierce, rage flooding through me like a wildfire I couldn't contain. There was nothing in the world I wanted more than to order him out of the kitchen and demand he never come back because, goddammit, he had no right. Clearly, the lines had been blurred around here. It might have been way past time to solidify some boundaries and refresh the staff on what I expected from them during working hours.

Otherwise, I would have no choice but to fire an exceptional sous chef for the crime of a crush on the woman currently driving me out of my goddamn mind.

8

CLAUDIA

Leave it to Sebastian to take something I'd been looking forward to and turn it into a pit in my stomach. He had a gift for that sort of thing.

Ever since Hadley offered to come out when we spoke last week, I had imagined the pleasure of showing her around the kitchen. The pride behind it. No, it wasn't mine, but it was impressive, and I was part of it. Something real, something better than a set on a television show.

Now? The last place I wanted to be was anywhere Sebastian breathed the same air. He couldn't have settled his problem with me in private? Where we might have come to an understanding and joined forces against an asshole calling herself a journalist.

But no. He chose to throw his weight around like a bull in a china shop. He chose to humiliate me.

"Oh, come on! You know I've been dying to see

what the kitchen is like." Hadley wasn't about to drop the subject, though I was pretty damn clear on how much I wished she would the morning of her first full day in Las Vegas. Folding her hands like she was praying, she added a pout for good measure. "Please?"

"I don't understand why it matters so much to you," I grumbled as we strode through her hotel lobby. Technically, it would be our hotel for the duration of her stay, something she had insisted on. *"I never get to see you as it is. It will be like an extended slumber party."* Even if I weren't cool with the idea, which I was, I would have gone along with it simply because I was so damn lonely out here. Everybody in the kitchen was nice, friendly, but that didn't mean we were friends. There was nobody to sit around with after work, comparing notes, commiserating over stressful situations we had navigated that night.

Kitchen workers were a rare breed. There weren't many people who could understand us—the schedule, the stress, the fact that we still loved it anyway. It took a special kind of person and maybe a healthy amount of self-loathing to sustain that kind of abuse.

But they all had their routines, habits, and hangouts. I only shone a spotlight on them. I would make things awkward for the crew if I tagged along and attracted unwanted attention from my remaining fans while they tried to hang out and unwind. Even now, today, I caught a few curious glances as we crossed the lobby, planning to grab a couple of iced lattes before Hadley spent a typical tourist day in town.

Stella assured me she had everything under control at the restaurant. We worked as a team the way people normally did when they'd known each other for years. That was a special sort of relationship, and I didn't take it for granted for a second.

"Come on." Hadley threw an arm around my shoulders once she finished pulling her long, strawberry blonde locks into a bun on top of her head. "Think of it this way. The big, bad wolf isn't going to blow your house down while I'm around. Right? He'll play nice in front of a stranger."

Sadly, she had a point. He would put on his warm, professional front for her sake, if for no other reason. He wouldn't make a jackass out of himself and put me on the spot.

Would he?

Either way, one thing was clear—she wasn't going to let it go. She never did once she set her mind on something. Rather than waste my time protesting, I shrugged as we moved closer to the head of the line at the coffee kiosk. "Fine," I grumbled. "Don't say I didn't warn you if he acts like a dick."

"Don't worry. I'll charm him." What I wouldn't give for her confidence. Instead, all I had was an annoying sense of dread as we rolled down the Strip in my new Honda. I wasn't interested in anything flashy—steadfast and reliable were the words I kept in mind when looking for a car. Another holdover from my youth, when so much of my daily life was in question.

While I drove, Hadley ran down the laundry list of things she wanted to do and see in town. "I want to do that crazy roller coaster thing on the top of the Strato," she raved. "You know, the one where they dangle you over the edge. You have to go with me."

"Argh, hard no!" I insisted, laughing uncomfortably at the idea of hanging off the edge of an almost nine-hundred-foot tower. "No way. That looks insane!"

"I know." Her eyes were shining when I looked her way to find her gazing in wonder at the sights lining both sides of the Strip. "That's what makes it so fun. Controlled panic. The illusion. Deep down inside, you know you're safe."

"I don't know any such thing," I replied while she groaned. "But I think it's cute you believe that."

"Boy. At least I know I don't have to worry about you gambling away all your money out here since you never take a chance on anything." I couldn't tell if she approved or not by the time we reached the restaurant, where work was underway to prepare for a busy Sunday night. Knowing I'd have tomorrow off and would be able to spend the day with Hadley without feeling guilty for missing time was a bright spot in an otherwise fairly awkward situation. It felt slightly shitty, letting my assistant take the reins.

Even if the timing couldn't have been better, it was an excuse to steer clear for a few days while things cooled down between Sebastian and me, and only going in if we fell behind or if Stella needed help but mostly keeping away from him. He didn't even seem to mind when I suggested spending time showing Hadley around town. If anything, he struck me as relieved, and that was before he'd bitched me out. He was probably glad he wouldn't have to look me in the eye after being rejected.

Please, Sebastian. Behave. I hadn't told Hadley about the backlash from the article, which was published in today's paper. Frankly, it wasn't nearly as bad as he wanted to make things out to be. There was plenty of innuendo, a few thinly veiled barbs, but nothing serious. For God's sake, it was the "Arts and Leisure" insert in the Sunday paper. Who the hell cared?

He did, the jerk. And rather than put the blame where it belonged, he heaped it on me. Because that was how he functioned. He never stopped to think. He just blamed the first person he found.

He sort of reminded me of my ex that way, which was not a compliment. Nowhere close.

My stomach was in knots by the time I parked, and we got out of the car. Sebastian's black Lamborghini was in its customary spot. Would it have been too much to ask him not to be here for a few minutes while I gave her a tour?

Here goes nothing.

I led her through the heavy door, waving at a few line cooks as we walked past the time clock and toward

Sebastian's office. The door was closed, granting me a measure of comfort. I could hope he'd be too busy to emerge from his tiny cave. "Everyone?" I called out. "This is my friend, Hadley. She's visiting from New York."

The chorus of greetings from the crew warmed my heart. It wasn't all misery and antagonism around here. That warm, wonderful feeling lasted all of three seconds before Sebastian's office door swung open so he could step out.

Dammit. Why did he have to stop my heart like he did, a day after he'd shouted me down like I was an unruly child? Looking ridiculously hot in a tailored white shirt, the top two buttons open to reveal a glimpse of a tanned throat and chest. His dark hair was slightly disheveled as if he'd been running his fingers through it while reviewing reports or whatever it was he did with the door closed. Hunger unfurled in me, leaving me longing to brush a strand of hair away from his forehead. Just a single touch.

Hadley basically choked on her tongue as he approached, all smiles and handshakes. "Hadley, is it?" he asked, avoiding looking my way in favor of gazing down at her like she was the only other person in the world. "I'm Sebastian Kennedy. It's a pleasure to meet you."

"The pleasure is all mine," she replied in a voice magically deeper than the one she'd used all morning, and over the past ten years we'd known each other.

"I'm so glad to have the chance to look at a real, thriving kitchen like this one."

"I'd be happy to show you around," he offered before finally acknowledging me. "If Claudia doesn't mind. I wouldn't want to take away the opportunity." *Your move*, he added silently, gray eyes narrowing—eyes I had to remind myself not to stare into for too long.

"By all means," I replied, wearing a parody of a smile. If he thought I wasn't following along, he had another thing coming. I wasn't about to leave my best friend in his clutches.

Even if she looked slightly disappointed as she walked beside him, oohing and aahing over such stunning discoveries as a food fryer, a row of ovens, a rack of pots and pans.

"This is really impressive." Hadley's hazel eyes shone as she gazed around the place. I couldn't help but feel proud, even if I didn't own it and had nothing to do with putting the whole thing together. I still worked here. I was making my mark slowly but surely, with or without Sebastian's help.

"We do what we can," he assured her with a twinkle in his eyes, wearing a smile that made me want to gag. Who did he think he was fooling? What, did he honestly believe I hadn't told her anything about him? She already knew about his volatile attitude, his quick temper, his inflexibility. Or did he think a charming smile and a few cute words erased all that?

The answer was simple. That was exactly what he believed, probably because he never had a reason not to. A couple of guys like him were on the show, thinking their faces and personalities could get them through when talent and perseverance couldn't. Sure, I knew more about him than I used to, and I understood him better, but that didn't excuse his jackass ways or how he'd embarrassed me so much yesterday.

There I was, swallowing all of that back, pushing it deep down inside me for the sake of playing nice in front of my friend.

"How come you're not wearing one of these white jackets?" Hadley asked, nodding toward Lucas and the line cooks he oversaw.

"I stepped down as head chef years ago," Sebastian explained while she gazed up at him like his words contained the wisdom of the world.

Glancing my way, Lucas grinned, and I returned it without thinking first. He was a nice guy, and I could tell he liked me, but there was no spark. At least, not on my end. He wouldn't force me to make things uncomfortable by asking him to lay off a little, would he? Nobody wanted to have the *'let's just be friends'* talk, especially when they had to deliver it to a coworker. It wasn't like I could avoid him.

"Boss?" Lucas raised a hand to get Sebastian's attention. He murmured a brief apology before peeling away from us to answer a question.

As soon as he did, Hadley grabbed my arm, her

nails sinking in until I hissed. "Sorry," she whispered, a little breathless. "He is fucking gorgeous! I mean, wow." She fanned herself discreetly, her head swinging from side to side as she looked around. "Is there an ice machine in here? I need to cool down."

Oh, no. Not this too. It wasn't enough I had to deal with his ego and habit of throwing blame all over the place? I had to stomach my best friend crushing on him? Flirting was one thing, but actively swooning?

"Girl, he's not worth it," I warned in a whisper, giving her a hard, serious look while she continued to overreact. "The man is a walking bundle of personality defects."

"But I can fix him," she joked. The problem was, I didn't think she was completely kidding.

"Whatever happened to the sensible girl who saw through Brandon and knew what a prick he was even when I didn't?" I whispered.

"She's horny," Hadley whispered back. "And she's only in town for a few more days. What's the harm in having a little fun?"

She had me there. I couldn't protest much harder without making myself look like a real idiot—a jealous one too. Pretty soon, she would start asking exactly what my reason was for being so deeply against her pursuing him, and unless I wanted to make up a story about him having a fetish for murdering women he slept with, there wasn't really a decent excuse I could offer.

Hell, I didn't even know why the idea disgusted me like it did. Not only that, but it made bitterness spread through me like rot, withering my love for her and replacing it with resentment. That was new. Never once in all the years we'd been friends, starting our first week in college when we were assigned roommates in the dorms, had I ever experienced a flash of bitterness over anything Hadley did. We were like sisters, the sort of relationship I'd never had before we met. She had never been anything but supportive, almost blindly so at times. The kind of best friend any girl would be lucky to have.

Listening to her giggle mindlessly over every little thing that came out of Sebastian's mouth once he continued the makeshift tour took me one step after another down a path I never wanted to travel. He wasn't worth this. So why did I find it so hard to keep from frowning and rolling my eyes, even coming close to scoffing once or twice when she made a big deal of complimenting simple things like the size of our pantry and the way it was organized? She was really stretching for praise.

I didn't realize until I was already halfway out of the pantry that Hadley and Sebastian had stayed behind. It was only when I heard her clear her throat that I paused, staring straight ahead while listening to what was happening behind me. "You know..." she ventured in a soft voice I'd heard many times while operating as her wingwoman, "... there are so many other things I would love to know about this business. Claudia has taught me so much about baking, but I didn't realize there was so much more to it until today."

"Did she teach you how to bake?" He was enjoying himself, the smug bastard, soaking up the attention like a dry sponge in a pool of water.

"Oh no," she told him with a high-pitched laugh that lit a fire in my chest. She was determined not to listen to me when I warned her about him.

What did I have to say to get through to her?

He was a bad idea, period.

End of story.

Only out for himself, which included whatever he wanted at the moment. After all, he had gone from almost kissing me to bitching me out in front of the rest of the kitchen. There was no such thing as loyalty, appreciation, any of it. Why would she want to be with someone like that, even as a one-night stand?

He would probably be incredible in bed.

As much as it boiled my insides to walk away, I had no choice. The alternative was listening to this awkward, extremely obvious mating dance while my brain turned to pudding and ran out of my ears.

Would he look at her the same way he had looked at me? Would he have the same light in his steel-gray eyes? Would her heart skip a beat the way mine had?

Would he remember her this time next week? He had so easily forgotten the moment we shared, after all. Something disturbingly close to disappointment made my heart sink and left me wondering if I should've let the moment carry us both away instead of doing the so-called smart thing and denying how much I wanted him.

"Your friend seems nice." Of course, Lucas was unaware of all this, slowing his speed as he came my way with a tablet in hand, where he'd listed everything that needed to be done before tonight. I was starting to think he went to bed with that thing balanced on his palm, the stylus in his other hand.

"Oh, she's the best," I replied. "I've known her for years. She's like my sister. I've really missed her." Even if I currently questioned her sanity.

"That's nice." It seemed like he had a thing for that word today. "What are you girls planning on doing tonight?"

Why hadn't they come back from the pantry yet? "Oh, I'm not sure," I replied, distracted. "There are tickets open for a few shows in town, and she keeps trying to convince me to go on that damn Strat ride that dangles you off the edge of the roof."

His face lit up. "Aww, do it! That's so fun!"

"Oh, please! Not you too!" We were still laughing when Hadley and Sebastian joined us, but suddenly, my heart wasn't in it anymore. Maybe it had something to do with how she winked, telling me she was feeling victorious, or how my core insisted on heating dangerously at the sight of him when he was acting all charming and witty.

What was wrong with me? I had never, ever begrudged her a flirtation or a hookup. Granted, we had generally gotten lucky because our taste in men usually ran along different lines.

But I wasn't interested in Sebastian. That wasn't the problem.

I wanted to protect her from him.

Right?

"I have an idea." Sebastian looked at Hadley, grinning, then turned to Lucas and me. What was he thinking? The gears were definitely turning inside that infuriatingly handsome head. "Hadley and I were planning on having dinner together tomorrow night. Why don't we make it a double date?"

Oh.

What the fuck?

It wasn't enough for him to dictate every move I made in the kitchen, he had to ask me out on Lucas' behalf now too. And he accused me of putting him on the spot? The idea of tearing his infuriatingly handsome head off and tossing it in the fryer was beginning to look a little too appealing.

Before I could even draw a breath, he added, "Claudia, you're rarely out of the kitchen for long enough to enjoy some of the city's nightlife. And Lucas, it's your night off too. Do you have plans? I would love to take everyone out to dinner."

The son of a bitch.

Hadley couldn't hide her disappointment, though

she tried. "Oh, that would be fun. I don't know, Claud, are you free?" I didn't need her to spell it out. She gave me a pleading look. *Say no. Please say no.*

Before I could, Lucas spoke up, "That sounds good. It's a really generous offer. Thank you," he told Sebastian, who waved it off like it was no big deal.

He knew exactly what he was doing. The snide grin he wore when our eyes met told me so. It was obvious he noticed the attention Lucas paid me. He could pretend all he wanted to extend an olive branch, but he was really putting me on the spot, making an already awkward situation infinitely worse by using the word 'date.'

"Sure," I decided, shrugging slightly when Hadley scowled at me. "That sounds like a good time." I could only hope Lucas didn't get the wrong idea.

Though, if he did, I would only have myself to blame. And I knew it. But that didn't stop me from rising to the challenge and taking the bait Sebastian dangled in front of me.

9

SEBASTIAN

We were roughly five minutes into dinner by the time I realized this was a mistake.

Not that it would've taken a genius to come to that conclusion before we ever sat down at Blush, one of a handful of independent restaurants in town that did not abide by the rule of closing on a Monday night. Some people couldn't afford it, while others liked to capitalize on the flow of diners who couldn't get a reservation anywhere else that didn't involve a corporate logo or a buffet.

"This place is gorgeous." Hadley was extremely complimentary, the way she'd been ever since we met up in the bar area to enjoy a couple of drinks while our table was being readied. Everything was gorgeous, amazing, stunning. She was trying much too hard to be likable, which struck me as odd since she seemed like she would have been very likable if she wasn't so determined to come on to me.

Which meant I needed to visit the doctor soon. Since when did I complain about a woman complimenting me? The touches to my knees and shoulders, the hand she occasionally brushed over my chest when laughing too hard at a joke that wasn't very funny in the first place. There weren't many things I disliked more than a hard sell, and that was exactly what she was going for.

Not that I had any room to be surprised. She had practically thrown herself at me like a fastball to the head in the kitchen yesterday. I was hardly unaccustomed to that kind of treatment, but for some reason, it felt different coming from her.

Probably because it so clearly irritated the hell out of Claudia.

Hence, we now sat down, the four of us around a square table near the center of the dining room. I had challenged her without coming straight out with it, offering this dinner, knowing she would crawl over broken glass before she would say no. Because at her core, we were the same. Much too competitive, too prideful, too intense.

I didn't imagine she would up the ante by looking extraordinary tonight in a simple, black wrap dress that accentuated her tiny waist and the full hips it flared into. She might have been petite, but she was every inch a curvy, enticing woman, especially with the addition of a little makeup and the attention she'd paid to her hair. I had seen her looking professional as well as completely casual on her day off. This was another version. Unfortunately, this version presented the challenge of keeping my dick from getting hard in public.

And dammit, I resented the hell out of her for it because Hadley was gorgeous—tall, willowy, with strawberry blonde locks that floated like a cloud around her shoulders. She was every inch the sophisticated New York woman, showing just enough skin to entice but holding enough back to keep a man wanting more.

At least, that was the case when it came to her sexy yet modest dress and sky-high heels. Her body language told another story. I couldn't remember the last time I'd asked a woman to keep her hands to herself, if ever, come to think of it, since it had never been a problem for me in the past. But sometimes, a man wanted to make the first move, and she was not interested in waiting.

I made a point of moving my leg out of her reach once we sat down, playing it off like I was too distracted by the menu to notice the attention. "I like what they're doing here," Lucas observed, glancing at me from over the top of the leather folder holding tonight's offerings. He had clearly taken pains to clean up tonight, looking much sharper than usual in a crisp dress shirt and slacks.

"Have you ever eaten here before?" I asked him,

and he shook his head. "I was well acquainted with the head chef years ago when we were both starting out."

"I didn't know that." He looked deeply interested, even setting the menu aside to turn his attention to me from across the square table. It may as well have been the two of us together, talking shop while Hadley practically stood on her head to get my attention.

"Oh, sure," I explained. "In fact, we considered opening a restaurant together."

Now, even Claudia seemed interested. "With Kristoff Darden?" she asked from my left, maybe a breath or two away from offering a disbelieving laugh from the sound of it.

"Is that so unbelievable?" I asked, my interest piqued for the first time tonight. The conversation until now had been interminable at best.

"Not unbelievable," she retorted. "Just surprising."

Angling my body toward hers, I tipped my head to the side. "How so?"

She arched an eyebrow. "How much time do you have?" A brief, playful smile tipped the corners of her mouth.

"Considering service seems a bit slow around here, it seems I have plenty." Like her, I arched an eyebrow. We could play this game all night if she wanted. I would win. I always won.

"Wow, all this backstory. Tell me more," Hadley offered, her elbows on the table, propping her chin on her hands. "I want to know everything about the genius restaurateur."

God, help me. I was barely able to withhold an eye roll. Rather than let her see the sourness I couldn't hide, I stayed focused on Claudia, who rolled her eyes while lifting her menu.

"There's not much to tell," I explained with a shrug. "We had a falling out." Over a woman I hadn't thought about in years, not until that very moment while trying not to demand Claudia tell me what the fuck that comment was supposed to mean.

"Oh, was it over a girl?" Hadley was now fully invested in the conversation while Claudia swirled what was left of the wine in her glass. When Lucas smiled her way, she returned it, but it didn't last long. *Damn, I need to stop watching her so closely.*

"Something like that," I admitted, but that was as far as I was willing to go. "Anyway, it was all for the best. He's been successful here, and I've had my success as well. Life has a way of working out the way it's meant to."

"I have a hard time believing the two of you could work well together. I'm sure you're right about it being for the best." Claudia had a way of turning what was probably supposed to sound empathetic into a blatant insult, and she did it with a smile.

"Oh, the two of you are well acquainted?" I asked with a smile roughly as genuine, meaning it was entirely fake. "I didn't know that. Otherwise, I'm not sure how you'd know about his working style or habits."

Lucas cleared his throat, reminding me to settle the fuck down. It was all her fault. This was who she turned me into. "Life pretty much always works out like it's supposed to."

"I agree." Hadley flashed a brilliant smile. "That's what I keep telling Claud."

"Oh, really?" I turned her way, setting down my menu in favor of giving her my attention. "How so?"

Though Claudia made a strangled, disapproving sound, Hadley would not be stopped. She had already put away two glasses of wine and was working on the third, so it seemed like she was hardly in the mood to pick up a hint when it was pretty much dropped in her lap.

"Well, she never imagined herself all the way out here in Las Vegas. We always used to imagine living together as big, established career women in Manhattan. But life has a way of doing what it wants, right?" she asked, wearing what looked like an almost regretful smile. Or sympathetic.

"What brought you out here in the first place?" I asked Claudia, pointedly ignoring her scowl. "I know what Sienna told me, but why was Las Vegas on the table in the first place? You were riding this wave of popularity."

"Oh, she didn't tell you about that?" Hadley asked.

"And I didn't intend to," Claudia warned in a sharp

tone, pairing her words with an unblinking stare. I took too much pleasure in getting under her skin, but even I would have stopped there if she looked at me that way.

Hadley, unfortunately, was having a little too much fun to notice. "Sometimes, a girl needs a new start when her fiancé goes and—"

"I'm hungry," Claudia announced, practically shouting the words to drown out her friend's voice. "Is everybody ready to order?"

Fiancé? I knew better than to stare, especially when she so pointedly avoided looking at any of us in favor of searching the room for the girl who'd presented our menus. "This pear and gorgonzola gnocchi looks delicious," she murmured, her voice trembling slightly. Was that pain I heard or simply anger? Did it make a difference? It was clearly something she hadn't meant to share.

Lucas looked apologetic, even reaching out to touch her arm at one point. She barely met his gaze, giving him the sort of look that was probably meant to reassure him, but it resembled a pained grimace more than anything else.

Luckily, someone provided a distraction from the discomfort. "Sebastian Kennedy." Kristoff Darden strode across the dining room, quietly greeting a few diners but quickly returning his attention to me. "I heard you were here with us tonight. What a pleasant surprise."

I took him in all at once. The same unruly, dark red curls, the same wiry frame he never could seem to bulk up no matter how hard he tried. His brown eyes glittered in a way that was anything but warm or friendly, no matter how he pretended otherwise. "Kristoff," I said with a smile, standing to shake his hand. "Allow me to introduce—"

"No need! We have a celebrity in the house." Kristoff took one of Claudia's hands in both of his, clasping tight, almost bending over her much smaller frame. "What a pleasure. I've been meaning to stop in and sample some of your work."

Then he turned to me, grimacing comically. "Then again, I understand there's nothing new happening over there, anyway. It's pretty much the same dessert menu as ever, right?"

Now I remembered why I hadn't made a point of visiting Kristoff's restaurant before now, and it wasn't only due to my hectic schedule. He was a man who took holding a grudge to new levels. He practically made a sport out of it.

"There have been some changes made," Claudia made a point of informing him with a gentle laugh. "You should stop in, sample for yourself. I, for one, am looking forward to seeing what your kitchen offers tonight. Your restaurant has been on my list ever since I got to town."

"How flattering." He then introduced himself to Hadley and Lucas, leaving me to stare at Claudia suspiciously. She caught me and lifted a shoulder. *What else was I supposed to say?* I looked down at my shoes, attempting to hide a smirk.

"Dinner's on me, folks," Kristoff informed us, holding up a hand in protest when I attempted to argue. "I won't hear of it. It isn't every day an old friend stops in and brings two beautiful women. You're classing up the place," he told them, making Hadley giggle while Claudia offered a brief, incredibly insincere smile. It was almost alarming how similarly our minds worked. I could almost forget how fucking irritated I was with her after that interview, not to mention all the other times she had managed to irk the shit out of me over the last few weeks.

"Oh, and best of luck with your new place," Kristoff added, shaking my hand again. "I'm looking forward to paying a visit once you've opened."

"Be sure to let me know when you plan to stop in so I can prepare something special for you." It wouldn't happen, but these were the things men in our position said to each other. As far as I knew, he'd never darkened Home's doorstep over the years. *Why start now?*

Claudia maintained a suspicious silence for the rest of the meal while Hadley chattered with Lucas about various preparation techniques and where they'd originated. The two of them seemed to get along well—maybe the night wasn't a complete loss for them.

"I haven't exactly been lucky in love, either,"

Hadley confessed to Lucas, who seemed amused if nothing else. "I've never been engaged like Claud has–"

Claudia cleared her throat and, if I wasn't mistaken, kicked Hadley under the table. "How about we don't talk about that?" she muttered, teeth clenched. "I'm trying to enjoy this cheesecake." As if to prove her point, she slid a mouthful between her lips, drawing my focus the way she'd done throughout our courses. I had never wished I could be a fork until tonight.

The sudden glance she threw my way damn near made my heart burst out of my chest. A jolt ran through me, something close to what I'd imagine an electric shock felt like. There was no embarrassment over being caught staring. No, I wanted her to know what she did to me. That, out of the two women seated at this table, it was her I wanted to take home.

Something in my face sparked something in hers. She set down her fork with a trembling hand. "Excuse me," she murmured, standing, her head swinging in all directions before she spotted a narrow hall in the back corner, where discreet signs announced the restrooms.

"I'll make sure she's okay." Hadley moved too fast, swaying after popping to her feet. "Oh, shit. I'm dizzy."

"Have some water," Lucas suggested, sliding her untouched glass closer.

"I'll check on her," I offered, already out of my chair before the sentence was complete. I couldn't bear the thought of her suffering. Something in me demanded I do something, anything, to ease the pain she was so clearly in.

It took a minute or two of waiting until the door swung open, and she emerged, her nose and cheeks pink like she might have shed a few tears. She stopped short on finding me waiting, her shoulders sinking. "Tell me you aren't waiting here for me." She sighed.

"Would that be a crime? Caring whether you're okay?"

"I'm fine." The way she sniffled told another story, as did the emotion hanging thick in her voice. "Thank you."

"I only wanted to help." Why was I defending myself? There was no reason to any more than there was a reason to flinch when she did. "You don't have to be embarrassed or anything." How fucking awkward. I wasn't helping a damn thing.

Instead of rubbing that in my face, a grunt burst out of her. "Have you ever wanted to keep one single thing about your life private?" She held up a finger in front of my face. "Just one thing for yourself after so much of your life was suddenly considered fair game? I couldn't even have that."

"Trust me." Closing my hand around hers, I lowered them both until they hung between us, still clasped. "You'll have plenty of life for yourself. There's still time to build it, and it'll belong only to you."

She released a long, silent breath, gazing up at me. I liked it almost too much. This moment, the two of us, the sense of her letting her guard down, allowing herself to be so vulnerable, I could almost see myself kissing off the lipstick she'd reapplied.

That was nothing new.

What was new was the way she leaned toward me, lips parting as I slowly lowered my head.

Until I caught sight of Lucas out of the corner of my eye. Dropping her hand, I turned to him. "I think Hadley needs to go," he murmured, giving Claudia an apologetic look. "She's in bad shape." The man's timing in the kitchen was impeccable, but not so much outside of it.

Minutes later, the four of us made our way outside. "But I wanted to go on that crazy ride that takes you *waaay* up into the air," Hadley reminded her, blinking hard as she tried to pull her friend into focus after drinking too much wine.

"Uh... not tonight," Claudia decided, guiding her to the car while Lucas and I followed. "Unless you want to puke all over yourself."

"You sure you don't need help?" It was clear Lucas felt left out, let down. I had wanted to punish him for having the audacity to think Claudia was available. I knew that now. It made me no better than a small, petty man like Kristoff, who had let jealousy over a woman I didn't want destroy a years-long friendship.

"No, we've been putting each other to bed like this for years now," Claudia assured us once I helped Hadley into the passenger seat of a small Honda after the valet brought the car around. Something durable, not flashy in the least, probably because she grew up the way she had.

Hadley gazed up at me, her hazel eyes unfocused as she swayed ever so slightly. "I shouldn't have drank so much wine," she confessed as if I didn't already know.

"It happens." Considering it brought an end to her incessant flirting, I wasn't unhappy that it had.

Until she leaned out through the open door and threw up on the pavement, mere inches from my shoes once I backed out of the way. Claudia groaned and hurried around from the driver's side, looking horrified. "Don't worry," I told her. "It all stayed outside the car."

"I'm sorry," Hadley whispered, tears on her cheeks. "I was nervous. I drank too much."

It looked like none of our evenings were ending as we'd hoped or imagined as Claudia closed the door, holding up crossed fingers while hustling back to the driver's door. "Wish me luck." She sighed, meeting my gaze over the car's roof before ducking inside.

It wasn't entirely a bad thing. Hadley had given me an excuse to get out of the evening without having to let her down gently.

If only things could be that simple with Claudia.

10

CLAUDIA

"I'm sorry. I'm so sorry."

"It's all right." I'd lost track of how many times I had to assure Hadley I didn't hate her after what happened back there. She was a grown woman. It wasn't like I felt I had to take responsibility for the things she did. I wasn't embarrassed.

If anything, I was too busy being relieved for embarrassment to play a role as I helped her go through the motions of changing into pajamas, then tucked her into bed with two bottles of water on the nightstand and a bottle of ibuprofen which I found in her bag.

"Get some sleep now," I murmured, stroking her hair back from her forehead. "You'll be fine."

"He probably thinks I'm a joke." It was the last thing she mumbled before closing her eyes with a pitiful groan.

Clearly, she was talking about Sebastian. Did he think she was a joke? And why did I care if he did? I only knew as I changed into a T-shirt and leggings that I was relieved to have an excuse to get out of there without turning Lucas down. The resentment I felt toward myself was nothing compared to what I felt toward Sebastian for pushing my hand.

But at the end of the day, I could have said no to the whole date idea. I hadn't. Part of me maybe wanted to see what Sebastian was like outside the restaurant, in the real world. When he wasn't strutting around like he was hot shit, I should've known he would have been the same asshole as ever.

Though he did try to comfort me. My blood warmed at the memory. What was that all about?

Hadley was out cold by the time I finished getting dressed and taking off my makeup. It was still barely ten o'clock, and I was usually working at this time of night. In other words, I was wide awake, feeling restless and troubled as I reviewed everything that went on at the restaurant.

If there was anybody Hadley should've apologized to, it was me. She might have thrown up in the vicinity of Sebastian's shoes, but she'd embarrassed the hell out of me by bringing up Brandon. I was not interested in having my personal life put on display like that in front of Sebastian, Lucas, or anybody. It should have been up to me to reveal those personal parts of my recent past. I loved Hadley, but she had a bad habit of drinking too much and letting her mouth run away from her. I had forgotten that. Silly me, thinking we were old enough and mature enough to avoid an awkward conversation where I would have to ask her to keep my personal life out of things.

It would have been bad enough had it not been for Sebastian's reaction—his sympathy. My body cringed at the memory, but it was the memory of how badly I wanted to let him comfort me that had my head in a fog as I sneaked out of the bedroom, closing the door softly, pacing the front room of the suite in a pointless attempt at working off some energy. The memory of him was so fresh, vivid. He was right there at the restaurant, almost hovering over me, and I was so tempted. My pulse fluttered when I recalled the light in his eyes and how overwhelmed he'd left me. I was breathless and unsure of myself and my principles, which hadn't seemed very important at that moment in the face of a craving for comfort. It had been too long since a man touched me so simply, yet lit my brain on fire.

My skull was going to crack in half if the memories didn't stop assaulting me. The questions. What if Lucas hadn't interrupted us? *What if, what if, what's the point of wondering?* Spinning on my heel, I paced the length of the room again. I didn't want to leave Hadley alone, but the idea of waiting around in front of the television until I finally felt sleepy made me want to scream. I was too worked up, uncomfortable in my own skin.

Back home—because I still thought of New York as home—I might have gone for a long walk on a night like this. I grew up there, so the idea of being out late alone didn't bother me. I could have done that now, but it would've meant mingling with tourists. I didn't really have the patience for them at the moment. Maybe I had used up all my patience while witnessing my best friend make a fool of herself and me.

Of course, there were also the meaningful looks Lucas kept shooting my way throughout the night. Dammit. I need to nip that in the bud if it wasn't already too late.

My mind was made up by the time I peeked into the bedroom to find Hadley snoring softly. She would be fine. Still, I sent her a text to let her know I was going for a drive and would be back soon.

While my phone was out, I decided to send another text, this one to Lucas. Sometimes, it was best to simply get tough jobs over with quickly instead of overthinking things.

Me: *Thanks for coming out tonight. I'm sorry things turned out the way they did.*

I hesitated, then added another line.

Me: *I hope you understand what I mean when I say I don't think we should be anything more than friends and coworkers.*

My thumb hit the arrow to send the message. I closed the app and released a shaky breath.

I then grabbed my purse and keys and headed out of the hotel, returning to the garage where I'd left my car and taking the now-familiar route to the restaurant. The one thing about staying at the hotel was not being able to bake when I couldn't sleep. Granted, I didn't have much of a kitchen at the apartment, but still, it was better than a hotel room with nothing but a coffee maker.

There was only one thing to be done on a night like this when I was so unsettled and unhappy. I needed to feel dough under my hands. I needed to make it submit to my will. It was the only thing that would at the moment.

So, of course, what did fate decide to do? How did the universe decide to laugh at me tonight? Simple. It made me drive all this way only to find a familiar Lamborghini already parked behind the kitchen.

What to do? I could leave, go back to the hotel, drive up and down the Strip until I ran out of gas, or I could haunt another restaurant to test out some of their desserts to get some ideas.

But dammit, I didn't want to run away. My pride reared its head right on schedule. The same pride that sent me all the way out here to avoid facing Brandon and Shelby and everybody who knew how they had crushed me. In other words, I wasn't exactly renowned for making smart decisions.

Which was why I pulled in next to the Lamborghini and parked, striding inside like the idiot I was. One thing Sebastian wouldn't do was force me into hiding. I had a right to be here and practice my work. "It's just me," I called out when I opened the door, in case he got the wrong idea. "Figured I'd come in and waste some ingredients while a certain somebody sleeps it off."

I didn't see him until I reached his office door, standing open so he could gaze out at me, almost sprawled in his chair, slouching slightly, thighs spread, a drink in one hand. He must have raided the bar before coming back here. His laptop was open with spreadsheets pulled up on the screen. "How did I know you would show up here?" he asked with a wry grin.

"I have no idea," I confessed, flustered, trying like hell to ignore the sudden fluttering of my pulse. Unlike me, he hadn't gone home to change before coming in. His suit jacket hung over the back of his chair.

He looked anything but relaxed, though, sitting with an almost rigid posture, gazing at me curiously. What was he thinking? Why hadn't I kept driving? "How is Hadley?" he asked, not unsympathetic.

"Horrified," I admitted. "She feels terrible about almost throwing up on you. She knows she embarrassed herself."

He shrugged it off. "I was more concerned with you at the time. Are you all right?"

Dammit. Why did he have to ask it like that? In that

tone of voice, so full of concern and intimacy. I shook it off and shrugged. "I'm fine."

His handsome face turned to something much harsher, harder. "Oh, for fuck's sake, you weren't fine at dinner." He slapped a hand against his desk and unfolded his tall body from the chair. So tall. So much bigger than me, intimidating enough that I backed away. He followed, leaving his office, matching me step for step. "Can we drop the subterfuge for once?"

As I watched, he pushed up his sleeves, revealing his corded muscles, and there went my pulse again. Something about him made even the most mundane actions seem relevant, exciting. "You were obviously upset back there. I was sorry your secret came out like it did."

"I wouldn't call it a secret, exactly." At the same time, my skin felt hotter and tighter than it did before, so much so that desperation made me walk away. I left him behind, heading for the walk-in, searching for cold butter. I was in the mood to create something. I needed something good to come out of this night.

Hell, I needed to cool off. A trip to a giant refrigerator was the only option.

"Then what would you call it?" He stood in the open doorway, blocking me until I rolled my eyes and heaved a sigh. Once he left enough room, I slid past, careful to avoid touching him. I almost succumbed to his touch earlier in the evening and wasn't going to take the risk.

Only once I reached the prep table did I remember he'd asked a question. What was it? "I call it my personal life, which is private."

He stood across from me, his palms on the stainless-steel surface, a smirk twisting his mouth. "The stupid asshole cheated on you, didn't he?"

My entire body cringed at the memory, but I forced myself to focus on the waxed paper wrapping around the butter. "I thought I just said my life was private."

"It's a simple question."

Oh, sure. So simple. He wanted answers? Fine. He'd get them. My head snapped up, and I felt heat rushing to my cheeks before I spat, "Yes. He did. With a friend of mine," I added, spitting out the word. "Or I thought she was. We were supposed to work together. Instead, I walked in on them fucking in my bed. All of a sudden, I developed a craving for desert life."

"He's a stupid bastard," he deadpanned.

"Would you look at that? Something we can agree on," I muttered. What the hell was I doing? This was all wrong. Being here with him like this, the energy in the air, the memories crowding in and filling me with longing. The sort of aching longing that followed loneliness. Rejection. They had made me feel so small and unwanted. Replaceable.

"Hey, look at me."

That was the problem. If I looked at him, I might not be able to stop looking. Wanting. Hating myself for being so needy. "I can't," I whispered.

"Why?" He was rounding the table, taking one slow step after another, making it impossible to breathe. "Are you so afraid of looking at someone who sees you as more than the girl who was on that cooking show once?"

"Don't joke about that." It was enough to make me look up at him, anyway, to steal the breath from my lungs when our gazes locked and forget everything I ever knew—who I was, what I wanted, what it would take to get it. None of that mattered in this moment with Sebastian staring into my soul and my battered heart skipping a beat.

"I don't understand what's happening," I whispered, searching for answers in his steely eyes. "I keep telling myself to stay away from you. So how am I here, like this?"

"You're asking the wrong person." He used both hands to brush my hair back from my face and tilt my head back so our mouths would align. His thumbs stroked my cheeks while he continued, "Because I was wondering the same thing. I only know I can't stand another minute without knowing what your mouth tastes like." His gaze lowered to my lips, his nostrils flared, and a soft groan stirred in his throat.

Was this a mistake? Did I care anymore about him touching me and staring into my soul? "You'd better find out," I whispered, straining upward to meet him.

He wasn't gentle. He did not take his time. No, instead, he claimed my mouth all at once, his kiss urgent, determined, sweeping aside any last lingering doubts in favor of pure sensation. The thrill of giving in, finally getting what I had refused to admit I wanted. Since when did my needs not matter?

God, there was so much of him! His hands were everywhere, lighting my body on fire, giving me no choice but to cling helplessly to him or else drop to the floor when my head started to spin. A whimper passed from my mouth to his, but he only responded by growling, wrapping his arms around me, and lifting me onto the table.

This was wrong. Not here, not now, even if nobody would show up for work until morning, but I wasn't about to try and stop it. I was through denying myself. Just this once, I would forget my goals and dreams and let myself go.

And I did that by allowing my hands roam over his chest and down his abs, reveling in his rippling muscles. But that wasn't enough, just like it wasn't enough for him to feel me up over my shirt and bra while nipping my bottom lip and thrusting his tongue against mine. With a frustrated grunt, I pulled my shirt over my head, squealing when he buried his face in my breasts, letting his lips and tongue explore my skin until I wrapped my legs around his hips and pulled him closer because, my God, the ache. It was too much.

His delicious, deep growl made my nerves sizzle before he used those big hands on my hips, pulling me close against his insane erection. Just as big as the rest of him, thick, demanding. My already hot, throbbing pussy tightened painfully, aching until I moved my hips in a vain attempt at relief.

"In such a hurry," he muttered, pulling down my lacy bra cup, taking my nipple in his mouth while rolling the other between his fingers.

"Yes," I whispered, running my fingers through his thick hair. "Yes, please." I didn't even know what I was saying. I only knew what I needed and wanted, and he could give it to me. He had exactly what it would take to wipe the slate clean. To make me forget.

I slid a hand between us, cupping him, craving his throaty growls against my skin. The sound of it was almost as good as the feel of him, his muscles working under his skin, skin I explored once I pulled his shirt free of his waistband. With a grunt, he tore it open, buttons popping off and skittering across the floor. "Touch me," he growled, dragging his fingers over my skin the way he wanted.

I had to, didn't I? I had to touch him to finally indulge in what I had craved for weeks. He was like chiseled granite but warm, real, and currently pressed against me.

He lowered me onto my back, and I sucked in a surprised breath at the cold metal against my hot skin. The sensation passed, replaced by the fire that spread through me as he kissed his way down my stomach, swirling his tongue around my navel before his fingers hooked around my leggings' waistband.

My God, this was happening. I was lifting my hips for him, helping him pull the fabric away from my body, letting him take my thong with him. I opened my eyes, parting my legs, watching as complete hunger washed over him. Greedy, animal hunger that made his ragged breaths come faster.

"So beautiful," he whispered, slowly lowering himself until he was on his knees. I couldn't believe my eyes. There he was, kneeling in front of me, propping my feet on his shoulders. There was no buildup, no teasing. He simply lowered his head and buried it in my pussy all at once.

"God!" I shouted into the silent room, my heart pounding out of my chest, my back arching. Too good, all of it. I couldn't handle it with the presence of his tongue in my folds, licking firmly, hungrily. His soft grunts of pleasure only pushed my pleasure further. Higher. My head rolled from side to side, and a chorus of helpless, guttural moans filled the air. All he did was hold me still, forcing me to take it, giving me more than anyone ever had.

It was happening. I was tightening, the tension in my core reaching its peak. "Yes!" I shouted, practically sobbing while my thighs tightened around his head. "Yes! I'm coming!"

And then I did, shaking in the aftermath, bliss radiating through me as the result of weeks of longing finally came to a head and faded away. Soon, there was nothing but sweet relief. *Why the hell did we wait so long for that?*

I was the only one relieved. The kisses he delivered to my inner thighs were just as hot, full of need. He was breathing harder than ever by the time he lifted his head. "I could live off your taste," he rasped, making me shiver. Who wouldn't want to hear that from a man like him?

"But what I really want to know is..." He reached into his back pocket and pulled out his wallet, leaving it on the table, and undid his belt. All the while, he held my gaze, forcing me to sink deeper under his spell. "Is this pussy as tight as I think it is?"

Again, I shivered in anticipation. Raising myself on my elbows, I watched, transfixed by the sight of him pulling his dick free from his boxer briefs. Holy fuck. Thick, with a wide head that oozed precum. Yes, my pussy would be tight when it came to getting fucked by something like that. The need was building in me again, hotter this time, all-consuming.

"What do you think?" He opened a foil packet and rolled the condom down to his base. "Should I try and find out?"

"You'd better," I told him, holding my breath, trembling as he dragged his head through my slit, so thick and wide.

So, so good once he breached my entrance and sank inside.

My head fell back, all of my focus trained on the

place where our bodies now met. He sank deeper, filling me, stretching me to my limit. All I could do was reach for him, my nails dragging across his skin, my body clenching around him. I locked my legs behind his ass, pulling him deeper, my body taking over and demanding what it wanted next.

With a dark, wicked chuckle, he took me by the hips and set his rhythm. "Tight…" he groaned, closing his eyes. "So fucking tight. So greedy. I can still feel you fluttering around me. You think you can give me another one?"

"Yes," I moaned. It was inevitable. There was no other way this could end, not with him working my body the way he did—grinding against me, rubbing his base against my clit, massaging me inside with every deep, sure stroke.

"That's good," he grunted, slamming himself hard enough to make me yelp while the table inched across the floor. "Because I want you to come on me. I want you to come with me inside you. Are you going to do that for me?"

"Yes!" I sobbed, already halfway there, not sure if I wanted to go on forever or if I couldn't wait for the explosion I knew was coming. "Yes!"

There were no more words after that. There was only sensation, ragged breathing, deep groans, my helpless moans drowning the rest of it out as he took me higher, further, with every sharp stroke. Faster, harder until there was nothing I could do but close my eyes and give myself over to him. To this.

"Yes, just like that... I'm coming... I'm... Sebastian!" A deep shudder ran through me when the tension broke. Oh, yes, that was good, that was perfect. Coming with him inside me, feeling every inch of him still moving, taking what I wanted so much to give.

But not for long since he picked up his pace, taking me hard, pounding me in the final moments before slamming deep one last time. I opened my eyes to find his eyes closed, the tendons standing out on his neck. Grunting through clenched teeth, he held himself in place for a few seconds, pulled out, and left me whimpering softly in the aftermath.

Holy shit. That just happened. In the kitchen. There was no way I could have imagined it being that explosive. Intense. It was like I had never been with a man until now. He was in a whole different league.

And it was not my league. Dammit. Why did the voice of reason have to sound off in my head at that particular moment? Couldn't I at least come down from my orgasm before reality started trickling in?

Then he smiled and made things so much worse because I wanted to smile back. I wanted to sit up and let him hold me.

Instead, I did sit up, only it was to adjust my bra and look on the floor for my clothes. "I need to sanitize this table," I murmured, unable to look at him for fear of what it would do to my heart.

"You can give yourself a second or two," he pointed out, chuckling softly as he pulled himself together. "I would say you owe me a shirt, but I ruined it myself. I guess that's what you do to me."

I didn't find it so funny. It was so easy for him to do this to me, wasn't it? I barely offered any resistance at all. And now he had leverage over me because he knew I wanted him. He had to know I would want this again, more than ever now that I knew how good it could be.

It meant being weak, leaving myself open to being hurt by him. I told myself it would never happen again, goddammit.

"I'm sorry about that," I managed, my throat tight. I would never be able to use this table now without thinking about what we had done. Stupid Claudia.

"Hey. There's no fire. You don't have to rush around," he reminded me with a laugh in his voice. When all I did was slide into my flats and head for the cleaning products, he stopped me, holding me in place when he took me by the hips from behind. "Claudia, come on. It doesn't have to be like this."

His lips brushed against my neck, and dear God, I wanted to lean against him. I wanted him again.

"Don't you see? That's why I can't do this." I forced myself to ignore the way his kiss made me shiver. I had to. One of us had to be smart, and it was the one of us who had the most to lose. "I got fucked over back home. I don't want that to happen again."

"Who says it would?"

"Nobody starts off to fuck somebody over. At least, I hope not." I finally managed to extricate myself from his grasp, turning in time to observe his crestfallen expression. It only made things worse. More difficult.

"You have a funny way of standing on your principles when you've already gotten what you wanted." He folded his arms over his open shirt, his eyes narrowing. "You can't take it back now. You can't pretend it didn't happen or that you didn't want it just as much as I did."

"I wasn't trying to pretend. I'm not going to lie. But that doesn't mean—"

"I know what it means. You can spare me." Holding up a hand, he backed away, repositioning the table, and heaved a heavy sigh of frustration. "I'll help you clean up."

"You don't have to." Because I only thought I knew what torture was while fighting to keep away from him. This was true torture, having to face him in the aftermath.

"Fine. Set the alarm." His soft grunt was the last thing I heard before he went to his office, wasting no time getting his things together and leaving me alone.

So I leaned against the table, closed my eyes, and asked myself what the hell was supposed to happen next while my body continued to tremble.

11

SEBASTIAN

"So what do you think? Have I covered the bases?"

I should have been paying full attention to Felix at a time like this, sitting in my office with an array of resumes spread across my desk. They symbolized weeks of work on his part to ensure my new kitchen was adequately staffed. He'd managed to pull some incredible talent, and I had to applaud his diligence when it came to recruiting.

"I'm impressed," I concluded, noting what seemed like relief from him. "I would like to meet them, of course, but if they're half as good in reality as they are on paper, I think we are in great shape."

Great shape like the woman who moved past my open door with a sack of flour balanced across her arms. My impulse was to help her. I was almost halfway out of my chair when I stopped myself, remembering she was a grown woman doing her job.

There were other people in the kitchen who could have helped her, anyway.

"Hello?" Felix rapped against the desk with his knuckles to gain my attention. "I know you're easily distracted, but try to give me your attention at a time like this, buddy."

I gave him my attention, all right, scowling until he grimaced like it hurt. "Give me something interesting to listen to, and you won't lose my attention," I snapped.

"I was saying we need to put together a timeline of getting these people in here to train before they move into the new kitchen." He pulled up the calendar on his tablet, scrolling through dates. "We're looking at another four weeks until the soft opening."

Only four weeks. It was unnerving how time had flown. That meant it had been almost four weeks since Claudia came into my life and effectively ended my ability to concentrate on anything but getting more of what I had already touched and tasted. There was no denying the pull she had over me or how fucking frustrating it was to see her in the days since we'd had sex and pretending like nothing happened. I knew it was for the best, but I didn't have to be happy about it.

"I would like to go into this with everyone on a friendly basis, at least," I mused, pushing thoughts of her aside for a minute.

Felix groaned. "I never thought I would say this, but maybe we need to do a—"

"Don't say a group activity," I warned.

"I know, I know, but it doesn't need to be corny. We're not doing team-building exercises and shit like that," he promised.

"What would we do, then?" I dreaded the answer.

"Actually, I have an idea." The gleam in Felix's eyes told me I might not like this, but I didn't stop him from getting up from his chair and sticking his head into the kitchen. "Claudia? Can you come here for a second?"

"What does she have to do with this?" I asked, playing down the fact that I liked the excuse to speak to her. We'd been going out of our way to avoid each other since Monday—not out of discomfort, though I was quite uncomfortable thanks to the semi I sported most of the time nowadays. I couldn't get her out of my head.

Seeing her now, looking nervous as she approached, meant playing pretend in front of Felix. He was oblivious to the way we deliberately avoided looking at each other, asking, "You know how when you were doing Best Baker, they had those scenes where you all would go out and do things together as a team?"

What a shame I hadn't known he had this in mind. I would have told him she didn't like talking about the competition. She wanted to be known for more than that. Now, she was a deer in headlights, blinking hard, looking at him in disbelief. "Sure. We had activities and stuff."

"Did it help? Getting to know each other, I mean?"

This, she seemed to consider seriously, folding her arms and leaning against the doorframe while gazing pensively up at the ceiling. "I think so," she decided. "Though it actually kind of sucked in a way because we got to be friendly and then had to compete against each other. You get close to people, and you end up having to say goodbye to them. It wasn't easy." The glance she threw my way held genuine sadness that stirred my sympathy.

That wasn't what this was about. Felix looked triumphant when he turned my way. "I think that's what we need to do with these new people. Get everybody offsite, engaged in some sort of activity or another, let them get to know each other."

Claudia exchanged glances with me. "It's not a bad idea," she admitted.

"Fine, but what do we do?" *I hated the idea.* Still, nobody was asking me to go on a scavenger hunt, and if they did, they could go fuck themselves because I didn't do shit like that.

"Off the top of my head?" Felix asked. "What about going to The Strat and doing the whole thrill-ride thing?"

A laugh burst out of me before Claudia had the chance to groan loudly. "I'm being haunted by that place." She sighed. "The universe will not be satisfied until I go on that damn coaster."

"It's not a coaster," he pointed out. "It just dangles

you over the edge of the building. There's also The Bigshot. That's the one where you get strapped into a chair, and they shoot you up a hundred and sixty feet at, like, forty-five miles an hour."

Claudia gulped. Even I felt a little nauseous by the time he finished describing it. "Nothing brings people together like fear and trauma," he concluded with a shrug.

The thing was, I couldn't argue with that. One of Felix's many talents was understanding the way people thought. It was what made him excellent at his job—staffing my restaurants, managing the investors, and maintaining relationships with vendors and suppliers. I couldn't have done it without him.

"Wow, that should be the tagline for the restaurant," Claudia mused. Felix burst out laughing, and I joined him, leading her to offer a grin. "I'm just saying. It would really bring people in."

"If it makes you feel any better..." I offered, "... we could wrap the day up with a show at Planet Hollywood. A good friend of mine cast and rehearsed the new show over there. He could score us a block of tickets with a few days lead time." I'd owe Jackson a favor after this, but it would be worth it.

"That would be fun!" Claudia looked much happier about that idea. "I could almost make it through that Bigshot thing if I knew I'd see a show afterward. I've been meaning to see what's out there at the different hotels, but my job sort of takes up a lot of my time."

"Your boss sounds like a real tyrant," I murmured with a smirk.

"Yeah, he can be a real bastard when he puts his mind to it," she agreed. "He has this thing about reacting before he thinks."

Sitting up straighter, I replied, "I heard you have a habit of bringing up issues that have already been resolved." I wasn't joking anymore, but then neither was she.

"Uh, I'll see myself out…" Felix grimaced comically, pulling me up short. What was I thinking, letting her get to me while we were in front of him?

"Thanks for your insight," I choked out, ignoring the way he eyed me while forcing a brief smile for the sake of playing nice.

"No problem." She wandered off, her voice ringing out with a question for Stella, and I reminded myself not to follow her progress with my gaze.

Felix, on the other hand, had no problem openly watching her walk away. "She's got a great ass," he said. "She can't be sampling a lot of what she bakes with an ass like that."

"I know you're not talking that way about the pastry chef you were dead set on bringing here to improve our image." Folding my arms hid my hands, now balled into fists. I did my best to affect a joking tone despite the tightening of my jaw and the sudden thudding of blood in my ears. "Because you let the wrong person hear you say something like that, and we have a whole other shit ton of problems on our hands."

And I already had enough problems. The ultimate cliché—a boss fucking his employee here in the kitchen, no less. It meant crossing countless lines and should have meant me avoiding the woman like I'd avoid the plague, but the concept was unthinkable. There was no choice but to clock her every move, to pick up on her every word, even in the midst of a dozen overlapping voices. Never had a woman challenged, fascinated, or tempted me the way she did. The fury she stirred in me had a way of exploding into undeniable passion.

It was addictive. Dangerously so.

"Gotcha. I'll keep my thoughts to myself. Good thing, too," he added as he stood. "You wouldn't want to hear them."

I held up a hand to stop him from leaving right away. "Everything's smooth with the construction? No more permit issues?"

"Smooth sailing at the moment, but let's not forget, we weren't aware of any issues before they reared their ugly heads, either. There was no warning." Scratching the back of his neck, he added, "I still can't get a straight answer on how it all went down."

Neither could Grayson, according to his latest update earlier that day. "We'll figure it out," I decided because there was no other option. "So long as construction is rolling again." In the end, we hadn't lost more than a day of work before everything was settled, but I very much had the feeling the goal wasn't so much setting us back as it was getting inside my head, making sure I knew everything could crumble at any time. There was nothing I could do about it.

It was not a pleasant thought to carry with me throughout the day as I drove down to the new site and watched the men at work. I needed to confirm for myself they were still at it. That things were moving forward.

Rather than call Jackson, I invited him for a drink later in the afternoon before asking for a favor. "Oh, no problem," he assured me with a grin while lifting a glass of scotch. "Here I was, thinking you needed something huge. I can score a block of tickets for you. No problem, especially if that sexy little blonde you've got working the ovens is involved."

"Watch it," I warned, and I wasn't playing. It took a conscious effort to loosen my grip on my glass.

"Just saying. She's hot," he mused while checking out the ass of a passing server in a short skirt.

"You think any woman with a cute ass and decent tits is hot," I sighed. If anything, his wandering eyes made it possible to laugh off his comments about Claudia. I wouldn't have to say anything that might start a fight. "Don't you have enough of that to look at while you're working?"

His brows knitted together in frustration. "Don't remind me."

"What happened?" I asked, glad to let him distract me with his problems so I wouldn't have to think about mine. Things weren't terrible at the moment—progress made at the new location, things moving smoothly at Home.

None of it did a thing to ease my frustration. I was as tense and cagey by the time we closed for the night as I'd been all day. There was no keeping my thoughts away from her for long. It got to the point where I waited for everyone else to leave, knowing she would stay around to play in the kitchen.

By the time I emerged from my office with only one thing in mind, she looked like she was also thinking about it. Her hand ran through her golden hair, leaving me to imagine my hand in her hair, holding tight to control her mouth's progress up and down my shaft.

Rather than indulge in those dark, needful impulses, I announced, "Jackson said the tickets won't be a problem."

Her brows lifted, her baby blues sparkling. "That's great! It'll be something to look forward to while my life is flashing before my eyes."

"Oh, come on," I cajoled with a smile as she went to her locker and hung up the white jacket she wore every night. The sleeveless tunic she wore over leggings shouldn't have turned me on, long and shapeless, but I was horny enough to hump a fire hydrant by now. "It'll be fun."

"So you say." She couldn't hide a small smile, though, ducking behind the open locker door like she was trying to hide it. "I can think of better ways to have fun."

"So can I," I agreed, my dick beginning to swell.

Straightening up, she shot me a warning look. "Behave yourself. I'm not trying to resanitize the prep table again." Her lips twitched in something dangerously close to a flirtatious grin, making me twitch.

"How about I offer to clean it this time?" I teased, shrugging when she rolled her eyes. "Who says we need to use the table? You need a more vivid imagination."

Folding her arms, she retorted, "My imagination is plenty vivid, thank you." Her narrow-eyed gaze traveled slowly over me, telling me more than she would admit.

"Oh? Tell me about it." My voice was tight, if only because I was struggling to keep from pinning her against the lockers and shoving my tongue down her throat for starters.

"I'm not sure you could handle it." A flush touched the apples of her cheeks before her teeth grazed her lip. *Fuck.*

"I think I'm the best judge of what I can and can't handle." Taking one step toward her, then another, I growled. "Hit me with your best shot, Granger."

She was going to until her face fell. "Fuck," she growled, closing her eyes after slamming the locker door. "I'm trying to make the smart move. To not fuck up a solid opportunity by letting whatever it is you do to me get in the way. Why does this have to be so impossible?"

"It doesn't have to be." There wasn't a chance in hell of keeping myself from reaching for her, placing my hands on her shoulders, tipping her chin upward, and gazing down at her beautiful face. "It can be fun. We were having fun a few seconds ago until your stubbornness got in the way."

Slipping from my grasp, she shook her head. "I thought we talked about this. I can't set myself up to get fucked over again."

"Who says you would?" I sighed. "Do you plan on never giving anyone a chance ever again? That's no way to live." Nor was it fair to make me pay for the sins of some stupid asshole with a wandering dick.

"Look who's talking about fear," she muttered.

"I'm not sure I understand." I thrust my hands into my pockets, curling them tight against the frustration beginning to build. Oh, who the hell was I kidding? I'd been frustrated for days, watching the forbidden fruit parade itself around in front of me after not allowing me to touch. "What could be so important that you refuse to acknowledge the way things are between us?"

"How are things between us?" With her head

tipped to the side, she narrowed her eyes. "I mean, maybe I need to be clued in since I'm the last to know."

I had wasted enough of my life listening to her feign ignorance. "Again, with the bullshit. Don't you see what a waste of time that is? I thought—"

"What did you think?" she nearly barked, her face flushing. "Oh, because we did it once, we can do it whenever you want? The door's always open? That's not how this works."

Holding up my hands, I groaned. "All right, I think you need to take a breath. I'm not interested in your editorializing."

No one but my kid sister had the nerve to roll her eyes at me with so much scorn. "You don't get it, do you? Or maybe you refuse to. This isn't something I can afford to screw around with. We're talking about my future. And now you know how I've been burned," she added, her voice softer, shaky. She recovered quickly, though, lifting her chin. "I already gave too much power to the wrong people who only stabbed me in the back and left me scrambling around, trying to figure out the aftermath. I am not going back to that."

Taking a deep breath, she added, "I cannot let anything get in the way of my goals ever again."

"So there's no room for anything else? Two people can't have a little fun, relieve a little stress after a long night in the kitchen? That's all I'm interested in, and you seemed interested too," I pointed out. "But no, because it might get in the way of what you want."

"That's pretty much it, yeah," she retorted. "Sorry if that's inconvenient, but you aren't the only person involved here. You've achieved your dream. You're not fighting or struggling anymore. I don't expect you to understand."

Not fighting, not struggling? She didn't have the first clue. "If I weren't struggling, I wouldn't have hired you."

A look of grim satisfaction touched her features, and then she nodded. "There we go," she whispered. "At least you can admit it, even if you don't want to."

Damn my mouth running away from me. That was not something I did or could afford to do, yet I couldn't seem to avoid it around her. "So you got burned," I countered, forcing myself to ignore her heaving chest and flashing eyes. "By all means, give up. Never take a chance again."

Her satisfaction deepened now, including a faint, knowing smile. "Look who's talking. You refuse to take chances because of something that happened to someone before you were born. Maybe take a look in the mirror the next time you want to criticize someone for being risk averse."

Things were going to get much uglier if they didn't end here and now. I felt it—the outrage bubbling in me, bitter resentment, the very childish but very palpable impulse to hurt her back, to reduce her to a crying wreck. That was beneath me, or so I'd believed until I met her.

She released a shuddering breath, looking down at the floor. "I'm leaving. Goodnight."

"Don't let the door hit you in the ass on the way out." Again, beneath me, but there was no way I could let her have the last word. That wasn't something I did.

Pain creased her forehead, made her chin quiver, but she left without another word.

Soon, I was alone, and I was glad of it.

Even if I found myself breathing deeply to inhale the lingering sweetness she left behind.

Even if I wished I could take back every word.

12

CLAUDIA

I was actually going to do this.

Had I lost my mind?

I must have because there I stood, my heart in my throat, my knees shaking as we gathered in front of The Strat.

At least I wasn't the only one shaking in my boots, so to speak. There was a lot of nervous laughter around me as current employees and new hires gathered together. We had started our day with lunch, one of those awkward events where people introduced themselves and shared a few words. Out of everyone seated at the mile-long table, it seemed like only Sebastian and I didn't need to say much about ourselves. It was more than a little unnerving, sitting with a bunch of strangers who thought they knew the first thing about me, all because they remembered me from a show.

Though if I had to come up with a certain subset of the population who would remember every detail of my appearance, it would be the people now joining together to take the elevator ride up to the top of the tower.

"Come on, everyone," Sebastian called out, almost paternal, gathering his flock together. "We have tickets, and we don't want to miss our time."

"Whose idea was it to eat before we did this?" My new assistant pastry chef whispered as we exchanged a tight, nervous grin. Marissa Cortez had an excellent resume and, evidently, a fear of heights to match mine. She shaded her dark eyes with one hand and tipped her head backward, trying to get a view of the top of the building towering high overhead. At least I wasn't the only one with doubts. We had something to bond over.

"I've done it a hundred times." Lucas clapped a hand over her shoulder and gave her a warm, reassuring smile. "I'll ride with you if you're scared."

We exchanged a look, and he offered a brief smile, but that was the end of it. He never did respond to my text, but the week-and-a-half since our so-called date had gone differently than the weeks preceding it. He was still friendly, helpful, supportive, but he was not overly attentive. There were no random touches to my shoulder in passing, no rubbing my back to comfort me in a stressful moment.

It was better that way. He didn't seem hurt or anything, and it was easier to get along as friendly coworkers than it was to manage his feelings.

Good thing, too, since I was now busy managing Sebastian's feelings, not to mention my own. It was a blessing, really, how busy he was preparing to open the new restaurant. There were barely three weeks left until the soft opening, meaning he rarely made himself available except first thing in the morning and late at night when most of the day's work had been wrapped up and the kitchen cleaned. Otherwise, he was overseeing last-minute issues, shoring up details with suppliers, meeting with his investors, and giving interviews to drum up interest in the new location.

And what happened as a result? Did I take advantage of the peace granted by his absence? Was I able to keep my head down, develop new recipes without him hovering over my shoulder with his rules and standards? Well, to a degree, yes. Mostly, though, I found myself wishing he was around, waiting for him to open the back door and charge the air around me simply by existing.

In other words, I needed to get a grip on myself. I couldn't have it both ways, keeping him at arm's length while longing for him.

Hadley had made me promise to take photos from up top since she had never made it during her visit. It didn't help that she was too hungover on her last day here when she spent most of her time hanging around in the hotel room.

The way I was feeling, I would be lucky if I didn't drop my phone before I managed to get a good shot, and I was still in the lobby. "Are you okay?" Stella noticed as I hesitated, lingering near the back of the group while we waited to go up on the elevator.

"Oh, fine. I just hate heights. And being scared. And moving too fast."

"Oh, then, by all means, you should definitely do this today." Winking, she inclined her head closer to mine and whispered, "Nobody will know if you don't go."

"That's not true." Sebastian would know, and for some reason, it meant way too much to do this and get it over with, if only to show him I could. How often had I accused him of being afraid or unwilling to try new things? I wasn't in the mood to be called a hypocrite.

It was only him waiting for the elevator now, along with Stella and me. He arched an eyebrow, his mouth twitching with humor—a silent challenge. I would end up regretting not going through with it. Damn him and my pride.

While I was at it, damn him for looking so good in a pair of jeans that so temptingly hugged his ass. Between them and a fitted black button-down with the sleeves rolled halfway up, I couldn't glance his way without blushing.

"If it makes you feel any better..." Stella offered as

we entered the elevator, "… we can go first. I'll sit with you, and we can get it over with."

"I was already planning on going in the first group," Sebastian added, though no one had asked. I stood between them and glanced up at him, scowling, so there was no secret as to how I was feeling. Sure, we were going to a show later, but I had to live through this first.

"I think you're right," I decided. "I want to go in the first group too. I want to get it over with."

"You need to sit up front," Sebastian insisted. God, he was enjoying this. Knowing how nervous I was, not bothering to hide his glee because he knew he was only doing it to prove a point. How did I know he knew? I just did because that was the kind of person he was. He got off on challenging me, seeing how far I would go for the sake of proving him wrong. I wished part of me didn't enjoy it as much as I did.

"I'll do this, but I am not sitting up front," I insisted, shaking my head firmly.

"Oh, come on. What's the point if you're not sitting at the very front end, with nothing between you and the world far below but the nose of the ride?" He was enjoying this way too much, the prick.

"Really, it's not such a big deal," Lucas told me once we joined up with the group on the observation deck, which in and of itself was pretty scary for me. I knew I was perfectly safe, but that didn't keep my stomach from dropping as I looked out over the city. It felt like I could see forever from up here.

“Really?” I asked. “You’re not just saying that?”

“No. You go forward four times, then you roll back. It gets a little steeper each time they send you forward,” he explained, waving a hand like it was nothing. “Really, there are scarier things to do up here. Like Insanity.”

He nodded to where people were strapping themselves into eight seats, all of which were suspended from what looked like a giant metal claw. I watched with my heart in my throat as that claw then extended over the edge of the deck, dangling the riders almost in thin air, spinning them around.

All things considered, I would take teeter-tottering a few times off the edge of the building. At least there would be a track underneath me.

“Okay. I’ll go first,” I announced, earning applause from everyone in earshot. Sebastian didn’t applaud, choosing instead to nod slowly, smirking a little before announcing he would ride next to me.

“What, afraid I’ll change my mind at the last second? You want to make sure you hold me to it?” My hands were shaking as I strapped myself in, and then one of the employees double-checked the harness lowered over my shoulders and locked in front of me.

“Maybe I just wanna hear you scream,” Sebastian murmured for my ears only. “It’s a sound I could get used to.” It was a good thing nobody was listening, just like it was a good thing I couldn't throw him off the side of the tower since we were both strapped in now. Of all the things I didn't need while fearing for my life, his infuriating hotness was right up at the top of the list.

He couldn't leave it there, either. His hand found my knee, out of sight of anyone behind us, and whispered, "A little fear can be hot, Granger." His gentle, teasing caress inched my dress higher, lighting a fire in my core and drenching my pussy, making my head spin in a way that had nothing to do with the ride. I looked his way, locking onto his knowing, intimate gaze. There was no hope of resisting him. Moments like this, I couldn't remember why I bothered trying.

A recorded voice advised us to keep our arms and legs inside the vehicle at all times. "Enjoy your ride!" the disembodied voice added.

"Easy for him to say," I muttered while Sebastian withdrew his hand, chuckling beside me.

"You've got this, Granger," he insisted. "If you can handle making a perfect Baked Alaska in a hundred-degree kitchen, you can do anything."

He shocked me out of my horror for a moment. "So you watched the show?"

"When there was nothing else on TV." He looked at me. I looked at him. I forgot to breathe.

And then we shot forward at a downward angle that made my heart drop. "Oh my God!" I screamed as we came to a sudden stop, pitched downward. Every ounce of me was sure I was about to keep going and fall through the open air.

But I didn't, the track angling upward this time, the vehicle rolling backward and coming to a sudden stop that jolted me back in the seat. Then we were off again, the angle steeper this time, and I squeezed my eyes shut when it all became too much.

"No!" Sebastian insisted, watching me rather than enjoying the view. "Eyes open! You need to see this."

"Already saw it, thanks. Doubt it's changed much." His laughter was lost in all of the laughing and shrieking going on behind us. My stomach did all kinds of insane things, lifting and dropping while one high-pitched shriek after another tore its way from my chest.

"Hold on!" Sebastian shouted, laughing. I wasn't fooled. He sounded nervous too. Maybe a little scared. But it was the good kind, the exhilarated kind. This time, when he touched my bare knee, I covered his hand with mine and inched it higher because, my God, what a rush.

By the time it was over, I was shaking again, but for a different reason. Adrenaline pumped through my system, flooding me with every rapid beat of my heart. The world around me was sharper, clearer. I had never felt so alive.

There was no way I could stand around and not do something about it. I spent too damn long trying to play it safe. Look where it got me now—wanting somebody with every fiber of my being but holding him at arm's length, thinking that would do something to help me forget, to make it easier. There was no such thing. All avoiding him did was make life that much more of a challenge. I was so tired of challenges.

The next group climbed in, adjusting their shoulder harnesses and belts. There was a lot of cheering, whistling, and plenty of encouragement shouted, meaning there was no one paying attention as I touched Sebastian's back, waiting until he looked down at me.

Whatever shone from my face changed something in his. "Yes?" he asked, arching an eyebrow while turning his full attention my way.

What was I supposed to say? How could I tell him what I was thinking, feeling, needing? I only needed one word, nearly whispered, so he would be the only one to hear. "Later." A slow smile spread over his gorgeous face with a slight nod, then turned back to watch the next group.

Shit. What have I done?

My attention was split throughout the rest of the outing until we found our seats in the theater at Planet Hollywood. Everyone was excited, laughing softly, almost giddy. Were we all so desperate for a day off? It was refreshing to be out of the kitchen.

My laughter was nervous more than anything. Sebastian sat at the other end of our row, engaged in conversation with Allie and a few of the other line cooks. When he wasn't acting like a pompous dick, he had a warm, amiable personality.

Yet the glance we shared as the lights went down was anything but friendly. The only warmth it inspired centered in my core and made my pussy throb. He wasn't about to let me forget what I had started earlier. I didn't want to.

The show was exciting—the lights, music, and dancers were top-notch. What a shame I could barely pay attention, especially when every glance down the row revealed Sebastian looking my way. He wasn't obvious about it, thank God, but he was definitely watching me from the corner of his eye while everyone in our row and the one in front of us sat riveted to the action onstage.

It was now or never. I waited until I was sure he was looking, then stood with my purse in hand. After holding his gaze for a beat, I headed through the doors at the back of the theater and followed the signs directing visitors to the nearby restrooms. My knees were shaking by the time I ducked inside the ladies' room, and my heart threatened to explode, but I kept going because there was nothing I had ever wanted more. Not a Michelin Star, not the title of *America's Best Baker*. The memory of Sebastian's hand stroking my knee was burned into my mind and refused to let me go.

But this? Sneaking off for a quickie? What was I doing? No, I didn't want to think about it. I wasn't going to make that mistake. I was going to act on my impulses. I was going to do it for me, not with my future goals in mind or any fear from the past holding me back. I was going to live in the moment again.

He didn't keep me waiting long, knocking softly at the door. I swung it open and pulled him inside. There was disbelieving laughter in his voice when he asked, "That's all it takes to get you going? A near-death experience?"

The thing was, yes, that was exactly what it had taken to make things abundantly clear. "You talk too much," I whispered, boosting myself onto the marble countertop beside the sink. Hiking my sundress up around my thighs got the point across, convincing him this was no joke, and a brief smile flashed across his face before he almost crashed against me.

This time, though, he pulled me down from the counter and turned me in place, bending me over it instead. I had the pleasure of watching him in the mirror, his face contorted by lust when just moments ago, he was laughing. His hot, greedy hands ran up my thighs, taking the dress with them until it was up around my waist. His caress was white-hot, yet it made me shiver with every stroke of his fingers over my ass.

"If I touch this pussy..." he whispered, meeting my gaze in the mirror, "... would it be wet? Hot and wet and excited?"

"God, yes," I whispered, arching my back, thrusting my ass into the air. It was true. Going on that ride had done something to me, something that needed to be capitalized on.

When he pulled my thong aside and dipped his fingers between my swollen, shaved lips, I had to bite the inside of my cheek to keep from shouting my approval. His hand covered my mouth, muffling what I couldn't hold back while he rubbed me with a quick, skilled rhythm that left me grinding against his fingers, desperately searching for release. I had never known a thrill like this. In public, where anybody could find us together, where they could walk in and witness him taking control of me. Control I so happily handed over.

"Filthy girl," he grunted, working his fingers inside me, strumming my clit with his thumb. My teeth sank into his finger, and he hissed before chuckling. "Hurt me," he invited, fucking me with two thick digits until I couldn't think or breathe and could do nothing but shatter in helpless abandon.

"Oh, good girl," he growled, working me slowly now, dragging it out before withdrawing his fingers. Fingers which he then held to my mouth while he took his hand away. "Taste yourself. Taste what I've tasted."

There was something profane about it—dirty—which could have been why I liked it so much. I extended my tongue, dragged it over his wet fingers, picking up my essence. Looking at his reflection, I saw longing etched in every line of his face in the way his gray eyes narrowed as he watched and the breaths that came through parted lips.

“Fuck me, please,” I begged, spreading my legs wider, pushing back against him. He had to before somebody found us. My heart raced, and fresh wetness leaked from me while I waited for him to get ready with a condom.

Thank God he covered my mouth again before impaling me, or else we would have been in trouble. As it was, there was no being silent, not in the face of the almost unbearable pleasure of having him inside me, moving hard, fast, grinding his teeth as he took me like an animal. So deep, so hard, rocking me back and forth in a quickening rhythm that made it impossible to do anything but give myself over to sheer, primal lust.

“Fuck... Claudia... tight...” he whispered, rutting now, losing his rhythm entirely. I didn’t care. I liked it. Watching him take me hard and fast, my pleasure doubling, tripling, leaving me pushing back against his strokes until we both went stiff. Still.

Then it broke, leaving me shuddering while he leaned against me for support. Incredible. Unreal.

But it was very real, wasn’t it? The proof was in every flutter of my pussy as my orgasm faded, the lingering taste of my juices on my tongue, and in the wicked light gleaming in Sebastian’s eyes. “Remind me to take you on the Bigshot next time,” he whispered, zipping his fly, washing his hands while wearing a sly grin. “And now, back to the show. Give me a minute before you follow.”

The thing was, I wouldn't have minded going on the Bigshot with him or on any other thrill ride. I wouldn't have minded experiencing the thrill of fucking like mad in a public restroom again, either. Not when the aftermath was so damn good.

Unexpected, inexplicable, but so good.

It seemed Sebastian Kennedy was determined to teach me all sorts of things about myself.

13

SEBASTIAN

The poached eggs I'd finished moments ago churned in my stomach, a sensation that left me wishing Grayson had presented his intel prior to our breakfast. I wouldn't have been able to swallow a bite once sheer, flaming rage lodged itself in my throat. My friends, seated around the table, waited silently for once as I reviewed the information his contacts had compiled on the saboteur fucking with my life.

"Are you sure about this?" Not that I doubted Grayson's expertise. He knew what he was doing, and he made a damn good living doing it. Years worth of high-paying clients couldn't be wrong. Still, the information he'd placed in front of me was alarming, and I wanted to be sure before I made a move.

"I'm going to try to not be insulted by that." He was grinning, though, and finally nodded in acknowledgment of my question. "Absolutely. That's Marissa

Cortez, your new assistant pastry chef. She worked for Kristoff Darden for four years. He put her through culinary school. According to the guys I had tailing him, they discussed their next steps while they were out together. She's his girl on the inside, a plant. This motherfucker has been after you for a while now."

Kristoff. I'd gone so long without thinking about him, without so much as considering him. Why would I? He wasn't my competition. I had no real competition.

Clearly, he felt differently. "So what's the story with this guy?" Aiden asked, glancing around the table like he wanted to be sure he wasn't the only one who couldn't remember where the bad blood between us had started.

"It all went down long ago before I met any of you," I explained, flipping through photos of Kristoff and the girl we had recently hired as a pastry assistant at the new location. I had observed Claudia and Stella chatting with her during the group activity a few days ago. I'd even noticed Lucas giving her a little extra attention. At the time, I was glad since it meant he had given up on Claudia.

The guy just couldn't catch a break since it seemed the girl was already taken. "These photos were shot recently?" I confirmed.

"Two days ago," he replied before lifting an eyebrow at Vaughn. "At Eastman Casino, of all places."

Kristoff and Marissa had canoodled quite a bit at

Vaughn's casino. He growled while reviewing a couple of the pictures taken while they'd gambled at his tables. "Oh, disgusting," he muttered, shaking his head. "I'm all about keeping the doors open to anyone looking for a good time and willing to spend money on it, but he's not welcome anymore. Fuck this guy."

I appreciated the solidarity but wasn't yet sure what I was supposed to do next. I knew what I wanted to do and exactly how much pain I would like to inflict on him while I did it. The words 'slow, prolonged torture' came to mind. There was a difference between what a man wished he could get away with and what he knew would land him in prison.

"He's got connections all over the city, but then you had to know that." Grayson continued, "He has friends in the union offices. Hence, the last-minute permit issues. He also knows people in the health department."

"The inspection," I muttered while my heart sank, cursing myself for not seeing it all much sooner. It was easy to say that now with the evidence laid bare in front of me. It all seemed so obvious. Someone with his penchant for holding a grudge would want to lash out once it was announced I would open a second location, thus confirming the success of Home.

He had never reached that level of success, no matter how fresh and exciting he tried to be. I had dined in his restaurant. If it hadn't been for trying to fend off Hadley's repeated touches, I might have fallen asleep. At least I had quality in my corner. People could call me boring all they wanted, but that didn't stop them from coming back for more.

"I know one thing," I decided, finishing my coffee with increased determination to get to the restaurant as quickly as possible. "I'm firing this little bitch first thing. Let her wonder why."

"There's nothing I like better than firing a traitor first thing in the morning," Vaughn joked, though there wasn't much humor in the situation. I appreciated him trying, as I appreciated everyone listening to my problems for the past forty-five minutes.

"If only it were that easy to fire lazy performers who are already under contract," Jackson grumbled, checked his phone, then stood. "Anyway, good luck. Tell that girl she owes me money for her ticket, whoever she is. I don't comp tickets for traitors."

We left the restaurant, chuckling, promising to keep in touch over this latest situation. We rarely got together at breakfast, but I had plans most evenings in the final days leading up to the soft open. Members of the press would be stopping in soon—photographers, reporters, providing foodies and an inside look at the new restaurant. We would run through the menu soon, inviting close friends and family to sample dishes before opening the doors to the public. The thought of it made my body tense in preparation, exhilarating me the way the ride at the top of The Strat had done.

But nothing could touch what came after. It was a

memory I had revisited often in the handful of days since but was smart enough not to bring up with Claudia. She had been out of her mind on adrenaline, buzzing on the thrill of conquering her fears, giving me the thrill of conquering her.

It was something pleasant to recall during the drive to work, where the top item of the day involved making a phone call the moment I reached my office without bothering to greet anyone first. Her number was in our system, and I punched it into my desk phone while wearing a grim smile. "Marissa?" I asked when she answered. "Sebastian Kennedy." Incredible, how non-murderous I sounded.

"Oh, hi!" she replied, chipper. "I wasn't due to come in until later today. Did I read the schedule wrong?"

She had read a lot of things wrong if she thought she was going to get away with her shit. There she was in the photos Grayson had provided, spread out on top of the folder he'd given me. Cuddling against Kristoff at a blackjack table, blinding herself around him as he played poker. I needed to stop looking at them before I screamed.

Bitterness flooded my veins, and at first, I could only grunt. "No. You're right about the schedule. Unfortunately, there's been a change of plans, and your services won't be required any longer."

She kept me waiting a beat, then another, before asking, "What do you mean? Why not? What did I do wrong?" Every word sent her voice rising in pitch until she was almost squeaking by the time she finished.

"Like I said, it's only a change in plans." *I don't employ women who've plotted against me while touching Darden's dick.* "You'll be compensated for the time you spent training."

"Please, Mr. Kennedy, if there's something I can do—"

"Best of luck in the future." I had to end it there. Otherwise, I would have tipped my hand by sending Kristoff my regards. For once, I was ahead of him. It would mark the first time since all of this began.

There was something else I needed to do, and this time, it came with mixed feelings. I couldn't help but crave the opportunity to have a few minutes alone with Claudia, an excuse to call her into my office, away from the rest of the crew. She might accuse me of trying to sneak around if there wasn't a solid reason for pulling her aside. My reasoning was certainly solid.

But I didn't crave worrying her. I didn't want her fretting over what Kristoff might and might not be planning next. I had every intention of burying him over this. He didn't have my resources and hadn't invested his money like I had. How did I know? I knew him. He liked his flashy cars, his nights out on the town. My lawyers could reduce him to nothing but a stain if that's what I told them to do.

I considered the words I would use, weighing my

options as I exited the office with Grayson's folder still out on the desk. "Claudia? Can I have a word?"

She raised her head from the supply list she was reviewing with Stella. The suspicion etched across her forehead and bracketing her mouth was obvious. "Be right back," she said, eyeing me skeptically as she approached.

My hands curled reflexively as I imagined reaching for her, touching her, even something as simple as a kiss against her forehead. That was a first, imagining something as simple and innocent as that when it came to a woman I was interested in. My wanting usually ran along simpler lines. Take, claim, fuck senseless.

Forcing myself to ignore the aroma of vanilla clinging to her, I folded my arms and hunched slightly, my head closer to hers. Rather than touch my lips to her skin, I murmured, "I had to let Marissa go."

Her head snapped back, dismay replacing suspicion. "What? Why?" Her voice was loud enough to grab the attention of the line cooks, all of whom slowed their chopping and slicing in favor of looking our way. One sharp glance from me changed their minds in a hurry.

"Let's talk about it." I nodded toward the open doorway beside me. "Quietly, please."

Her feet might as well have grown roots binding her to the floor, the stubborn little thing. "No, hang on a second. The time to talk about this was before you decided to fire someone I've already spent hours training, developing camaraderie. Wasn't that the point? I wasted all that time."

My teeth would crack soon if I didn't stop grinding them. Why did she have to do this now? "And had I known then what I know now, you would not have wasted your time," I grunted. "Having a discussion before I called her would not have changed a damn thing. The result would have been the same." By now, everyone was paying attention while pretending not to. I couldn't announce this in front of all of them. They didn't need to know about Kristoff and Marissa. The fewer people aware, the better.

Stepping aside, I motioned toward the inside of my office with one arm. "In here. Privately. I'm not going to ask again."

Her hair stood out like gold against her tomato-red complexion. "You know what? I need to cover for all the work my former assistant was supposed to get done today." Heaving a sigh, she backed away, raising her hands in the air. "I'll talk to you later about it. Unbelievable."

She had no idea how unbelievable it all was. I could hardly wait to make her eat her words. Eventually, she was going to learn I knew what I was doing. Just who gave her the impression this was her restaurant?

It was almost a relief to have a handful of calls to make regarding the upcoming opening. Felix checked in to update me on the status of new prospects for Marissa's position. He swore there were two or three others he had passed on who boasted similar credentials.

"Do something for me," I added before he could end the call. "Go through the resumes. Find out how many of the applicants once worked for Darden." Because there was no guarantee I would have chosen Marissa. He would have sent more than one spy to improve his odds of success.

"I cannot fucking believe he pulled that over on me," Felix groaned.

"You didn't know to look for it. Neither did I." That was as close to understanding as he was going to get from me, and he knew it after years of working together.

Things got busy enough as the day went on that I wound up rolling up my sleeves and pitching in, pulling trays of bread from the oven, assembling baskets, plating desserts. The hours melted away. It had been a long time since I was in the trenches, shoulder to shoulder, working toward a common goal. "Behind you," I called out, carrying a tray of tart shells to be filled. I didn't mind the way my pulse pounded. It was a new challenge, and I had always loved a challenge.

It wasn't until service ended and the last customers left that I was able to come down from the dizzying high, the adrenaline rush. "Behind," Claudia muttered as she passed with a tray of cake pans fresh from the oven. “This, plus the tray now in the oven, brings us up to count for tomorrow.” She managed to announce all of that without a glance my way.

“Wow. I thought you forgot how to speak to me,” I murmured while everyone was busy cleaning, distracted.

“Let’s get something straight,” she hissed. “Just because you worked with the rest of us grunts tonight doesn’t mean everything’s okay between us. Got it?”

I had no choice but to hold back with so many eyes and ears around us. She would see, and she’d be sorry for jumping to conclusions. The kitchen thinned out before long, the crew leaving one and two at a time. I overheard a few of them talking about getting a drink later, but Claudia politely declined when they opened the invitation to her.

“I’ve still got cake in the oven, you slackers,” she joked. She paired that with a glance my way, though. I wasn’t sure she noticed she looked at me. It was probably subconscious, but it got the point across.

What a relief when only the two of us were left in the otherwise silent room, meaning I didn’t have to hold back any longer. “This is my restaurant,” I reminded her as she checked the oven timer. “I decide who stays and who goes. End of discussion.”

“Could you at least give me the benefit of a heads-up the next time something like this is happening?” she spat, hands on her hips. The girl could glare holes through a man, and she did then, her blue eyes glittering. "Maybe I could've taken care of it myself, given her a call. I'm the one who spent the past two weeks with her."

"Trust me," I said with a laugh. "I don't give a shit how she took the news, and she didn't deserve any comforting."

Throwing her hands into the air, she released a laugh like mine. "What did she do? Steal something?" She shook her head while swinging the oven doors open, grabbing a towel that was sitting on the prep table to withdraw the tray of finished cakes. "Because honestly, I can't imagine... *fuck*!"

The tray crashed to the floor with a deafening clatter, cake pans sliding over the tile like burning hockey pucks while Claudia grasped her right wrist. "The fucking towel was damp! I didn't notice!" she howled, eyes squeezed shut. Her palm and the pads of her fingers were already turning a bright red color.

Immediately, I took her by the shoulders and steered her to the sink, where I turned on the cold tap and placed her hand underneath the running water. She sucked in one shaking breath after another until I urged, "Breathe slowly. The faster you breathe, the worse the pain is. Calm your nervous system."

"Easy for you to say," she replied through gritted teeth. "Dammit, that was so stupid."

"I'm sorry," I offered, wincing at the way she winced. "I distracted you."

"Forget about me," she grumbled. "Take care of the cakes."

She would be more concerned about them than about herself at a time like this. I closed the oven doors before finding dry potholders and picking the cake pans up off the floor. Half of them had flipped upside down, their contents falling out and leaving me with a mess to clean up. It was either that or hovering over her, helpless.

While I worked to clean the chocolate from the floor, she continued, "Anyway, it was my fault. I know better than to be so careless." I looked over to find her grimacing as she examined the burn.

"Under the water," I grunted. "That's an order. I know we have aloe gel around here somewhere. It'll take the pain away."

"I have burned myself before, you know." The fight was gone from her voice now. She was softer, a little tremulous, and the sound did something to me that few things could. I had to help her. I had to take the pain away.

There was a bottle of gel in the first-aid kit, and I took it to her along with gauze, tape, and a couple of clean towels once I'd finished washing the floor. "Let me help you," I urged, checking the clock to make sure she'd had her hand under the water for roughly ten minutes before washing my hands and shutting off the faucet. She winced her way through to me, gently blotting the reddened skin dry. "You might end up with a blister on your palm."

"Hooray. I'm so looking forward to it. And it's in such a convenient place too," she added. I glanced up from where I squeezed the gel onto the wounds to find a tear rolling down her cheek. "I mean, it's not like I ever use my right hand for every single thing I ever do."

"I should take you to the hospital, have them bandage you up."

"No," she insisted with a sniffle. "It's not that serious. But thank you. I'm just frustrated."

"Is the gel helping?" I asked, gently wrapping gauze around her hand until it looked like she was wearing a glove.

Her head bobbed while a brief, shaky smile appeared. "It really is like it's sucking the heat out. Thank you."

I looked up from her hand to find her looking at me, her eyes shining with tears, brows drawn together in pain. The thought of leaving her in pain overnight made everything in me rear up in protest. "Do something for me," I whispered, catching one of her warm tears on my thumb. "Spend the night at my house. At least let me take care of you so you don't have to use this hand. It's going to hurt like hell."

"I'm a big girl. I can handle myself."

Was she? From where I was standing, she looked

vulnerable. Fragile. Pained. "Do yourself a favor and say yes," I urged softly, letting her draw me in whether or not she meant to. The fact that she leaned in, straining upward, told me she was with me. Wanting, craving.

"This isn't fair." I sensed the indecision she wrestled with and wished she would stop wrestling already. Didn't she see it wasn't worth it? There was no point.

"What isn't fair?" I asked, allowing my nose to touch her hair so I could inhale the sweet vanilla aroma like a dessert I longed to take a bite of.

"This doesn't mean things are any different," she insisted, even as she closed her eyes and swayed into me. "They can't be. Please, I know what we've already done, but—"

"Listen to me." I couldn't wait through another second of her denying herself what she wanted most. A slight brush of my lips against hers left me shuddering as every last ounce of my control drained away. "I know what you're afraid of, and I understand. I'm telling you that you don't have to be afraid."

"That's easy for you to say." She parted her lips, her tongue sliding out to touch mine before our mouths met, and I wrapped an arm around her to crush her against me.

"Come home with me," I whispered between kisses, going in for one taste after another. I couldn't get enough. "Let me make this up to you, no strings attached. But I cannot pretend another minute I don't want you. It seems like that's all I can do anymore."

The words came straight from my core and my cock, rigid, straining. Every soft, helpless sigh that came from her made me more determined.

"Okay," she eventually sighed. "I think I'd like to be taken care of..."

"But not just by anyone?" I questioned, finding the will to pull away from her. For some reason, I needed to know this meant more to her than just fucking.

Her teeth grazed her lower lip as she hesitated with a response. "No. Not just anyone."

14

CLAUDIA

"It's not much, but it's home." Sebastian stepped back after unlocking his front door, allowing me to walk inside and look at the beautiful two-story, Mediterranean-style home he so jokingly downplayed.

I immediately looked past the wide, airy foyer, searching for one room in particular. "What's the kitchen like?" I asked, almost champing at the bit to look at it.

"I knew you would ask." With an arm around my waist, he led me past the stairs, down a wide hall to what appeared to be a study and a living room positioned across from each other, and then the hall opened onto a large, sparkling kitchen.

"Wow." Envy swelled in my chest as I admired the expensive La Cornue stove, the gleaming copper pots and pans hanging from a rack over a wide, marble-topped island. The dual ovens and pizza oven could be used both from inside the kitchen and the outdoor kitchen, which sat on the other side of a pair of French doors. I could imagine him out there, entertaining guests, being the caring host he always was. I had come to understand that was one of his gifts.

"What do you think?" he asked, and the earnestness in the question was touching.

"It's gorgeous. What I couldn't accomplish in a room like this." It made my pitiful little kitchen apartment look like a joke. I really needed to move into a bigger place so I could practice at home.

"I hoped you would think so." He slid out of his suit jacket and draped it over his arm before looking me up and down. "What do you need? How can I help you?"

The insistence in his question warmed my heart and made me glad I accepted his invitation. "Really. My hand is not all that bad." I was lying—it still hurt like hell, making even the slightest movement send bolts of agony through my arm. Why did I want to make him feel better? Probably because he'd been so stricken when I got hurt.

"If you say that one more time, I'm going to tape your mouth shut."

"You have to be able to guess how many times I've burned myself. Look at your hands," I pointed out, eyeing a few faded scars still visible there. "You've spent enough time in kitchens to know."

"You are my pastry chef, and as you know, we are now short a staff member. I don't want you using this hand tonight, and considering you're right-handed..." His arched expression brought to mind a prosecutor who just finished making his closing argument.

"Exactly what do you think you're going to do for me?" Like I needed to ask. Like I didn't know long before his eyes took on a wicked gleam, turning them from gray to shining steel.

"For starters?" He looked me up and down and made a disapproving face. "You need to wash up after the kind of busy night we had."

A ripple of anticipation zigzagged through me, making me forget my hand for a second. It might as well have not been attached to my body, thanks to how he looked at me with so much promise in those gray depths.

"And I guess that means you're going to help me?" I asked, arching an eyebrow.

"Oh, I'm looking forward to it. I think you need a bath," he decided. "That way, you can keep your hand dry."

I had to be imagining this, right? Sebastian Kennedy giving me a bath? Curiosity convinced me to follow him, if nothing else, trailing behind as he led the way up the winding staircase. It was a beautiful house but somehow less lavish than I'd expected. Then again, he did live alone. "You should have your family dinners here," I mused. "Put that beautiful kitchen to use."

"I know you're right, but they like checking up on

me at work." *Right.* To make sure he wasn't working himself to literal death. "Anyway, I like the family feel at the restaurant. That's all I've ever wanted."

I'd never heard him talk this openly about his vision. Yes, he wanted to pay homage to his grandfather, but what else?

"I want the sort of restaurant where people can come in and feel like they're at home. I know, revolutionary," he added, chuckling at himself once we reached the second floor with its simple, clean decor. A few tasteful prints on the walls depicting what looked like Italian landscapes added warmth. "That would be why I chose the name. There is nothing in the world like walking into a restaurant and feeling like they know you, feeling comfortable, wanting to have big meals there with the people who matter most. That's a beautiful thing, and I don't take it for granted... the trust people put in me."

We entered a large bathroom decorated in shades of cream and forest green. I marveled silently at the large tub, which he filled with water that soon began to send steam billowing into the air. It was more than big enough for the two of us. Was that what he had in mind?

"Not too hot," I warned. "I'm already burned."

"Don't worry. I'll take care of you." Yes, that was what this was all about, right? Him wanting to take care of me. All it took was a dumb move on my part, acting without thinking, to send his protectiveness into overdrive.

Pretty soon, it was obvious I would need help since the simple act of getting undressed was a challenge with one hand wrapped in gauze. He helped without being asked. Gently, he pulled down my linen pants and lifted my shirt over my head. Somehow, he managed to keep things impersonal until it came time to unhook my bra. The hitching of his breath told the whole story, that and the stampeding of my heart at the intimacy of it all. It was too easy to fall under his spell, especially when his hungry gaze crawled over me the way it did, watching my every move. There was a sudden charge in the air, the way it felt before a thunderstorm, like lightning could strike at any second.

Once I was naked, he helped me carefully into the tub, where the warm water slowly enveloped me as I settled back. He even folded a towel to place under my neck so I would be more comfortable. "Thank you," I nearly purred as the water's warmth seeped into my muscles.

Unbuttoning his crisp white shirt, he said, "If you don't mind, I'm going to rinse off too." *Mind?* Who would mind the pleasure of watching him strip down? Should I have ogled his body the way I did? I couldn't help it. Besides, something told me he didn't mind. He had done the same to me, after all.

Soon, I was almost able to forget the persistent throbbing in my hand. It was much more interesting to watch him step into the shower stall and soap himself up. I forgot how to breathe as I watched the sudsy water slide over his skin, taking what was already so finely chiseled and making it look otherworldly. He couldn't be real, but he was, and he was directly in front of me. *Wanting me.*

By the time he finished, it wasn't just my hand that throbbed. My clit was in serious need of attention, too, and my nipples were tight enough to ache.

"What was that meant to be?" I asked with a smile. "Something to whet my appetite?"

"If it did, I'm glad. If you can think of anything besides that burn, I must be doing something right." The open confidence in his voice brought a flush to my face, even though there was nothing to be embarrassed about. He knew I wanted him. I had made it clear.

And he wanted me.

There was no question.

All the hate and back-and-forth had brewed a few weeks' worth of angry frustration, but beneath it all was a need neither of us realized was there—just like there was no question about whether I was strong enough to resist openly admiring the twitch of his bulge beneath the towel slung low around his waist. It sat low on his hips, teasing at the V-shaped ridge of muscles leading down to what thickened and swelled in front of him.

"How's it going over here?" he asked, gazing down

the length of my body and then kneeling beside the tub.

"I was hoping for a little help," I murmured, my heart thudding as he dipped a washcloth into the water and poured body wash over it.

"I'll see what I can do." At first, he was gentle but efficient, running the soapy cloth over my shoulders, neck, and throat. I closed my eyes, letting myself feel it completely, with no thoughts or reservations in the way. I was too happy to feel good while he took a tour of my body like he hadn't yet done. Every inch of me, or at least what he could reach, even lifting my legs one at a time and washing them from the tip of my toes to the top of my thighs without saying a word. It was enough for him to concentrate on his work.

I finally opened my eyes once he was finished with that, and I found plain desire swirling in his. There was only one part of me he hadn't taken care of yet, and I parted my thighs in silent invitation.

"It is essential I clean everywhere, Granger," he whispered, soaping the cloth again, starting at the place where my thigh emerged from the water and slowly, inch by inch, descending under the surface.

My back arched, and a low moan stirred in my chest. "That's good," I whispered, holding my breath, straining. I needed this too much, with all of my body and soul. I needed the sort of oblivion only he could bring.

"Relax." His voice was velvet, brushing against my

ears as softly as his hand brushed me underwater. "I'll take my time with you... make you forget everything else but me."

At first, he moved the cloth over me slowly, taking his time, each stroke torturously drawn out. But after a while, the patience wore thin, and his restraint gave way as he finally shifted my legs, leaving no room for hesitation and parting my lips with his fingers. "Oh!" I groaned. The electricity of his touch paired with his quicker, ragged breathing, betrayed his need while he took care of mine. I gasped and shuttered, jerking my hips to meet his skillful touch, whimpering my approval when he toyed with the aching, burning bundle of nerves.

"So fucking beautiful like this." He teased my earlobe with his tongue before grazing it with his teeth and doubling the unspeakable pleasure tearing me apart. "Are you going to give it to me? Are you going to let me hear you fucking scream?"

I didn't have a choice. There was no holding back, not that I wanted to. I wanted all of it, every ounce of sensation, every sizzling thrill his touch brought to my body. For one brief, breathless moment, it occurred to me I had lived all my life without this, and the thought was almost enough to bring tears to my eyes as I climbed higher and higher.

"Let go," he demanded, his breath coming hot and fast. "Come for me so I can fuck you. Don't you want that? Don't you want me to fuck you?"

"Yes!" I pleaded, not caring anymore about my pride. Nothing mattered but this. Getting what I wanted. Getting *him*.

And when I did come, shattering into a million pieces, he groaned softly in approval. "That feel good?" I could only moan in affirmation while he stood and grabbed another big, fluffy towel. Rather than helping me from the tub so I could dry off, he stood me up, wrapped the towel around me, and then lifted me across his arms.

"What are you doing?" I asked, still a little dizzy, a little breathless.

He got straight to the point. "Taking you to bed so I can make good on my promise."

This was a night of firsts—being bathed by Sebastian and now lying back against his padded headboard while he rubbed my feet post-sex. Was my hand still throbbing? Quite a bit. It was almost the last thing on my mind, though.

And if a burned hand meant this kind of treatment, while it was painful and annoying, it was almost worth it. He was at his most relaxed, dressed in nothing but a pair of boxer briefs, his dark hair nearly black as it slowly dried. I had the pleasure of admiring his chest, broad shoulders, thighs, and calves. The man was a walking ode to the male form and might have been proof there was a God. Or maybe that was all the endorphins running through my system, thanks to him.

"Oh, right there," I whispered, my head falling back when he applied pressure to my arch with his thumbs. "How the hell are you so good at this?"

"You don't know by now? I'm good at everything." I twitched my foot playfully like I was going to kick him, and he only laughed.

"I can think of a couple of things you're not good at..." I couldn't help it, I had to say it. "Like communication." There were still unresolved issues that not even the best foot rub could erase. "Are you ever going to tell me what today was about? Don't you trust me yet?"

"Don't you trust me?" he countered, making me groan in frustration rather than pleasure. He always had a comeback, didn't he?

"Really. Consider it curiosity," I insisted, adjusting the sheet over my naked body while leaving my legs bare. "What happened? I'm never going to let this go until you tell me. I'm just warning you now."

With a sigh, he switched feet, taking his time before asking, "Remember when we went to dinner? You met Kristoff Darden." He was clearly troubled, his voice deeper and quieter than previously.

The memory brought to mind a used car salesman. The guy had struck me as being roughly that sincere. "Sure. What does that have to do with anything?"

"As it turns out, Marissa worked for Kristoff. He put her through culinary school."

Interesting, but still. "I'm lost. What does that have to do with anything?"

"A friend of mine did some digging for me as a favor. He managed to make a few connections between Kristoff and the sabotage that's been going on... the surprise inspection, the issues with the union permits. I wouldn't be surprised if he started the rumors about food poisoning. And it all started after I announced the expansion."

Now I felt sick because it was all so clear. "You're afraid Marissa was sent in to spy on you or sabotage you," I concluded after taking a deep breath to calm the sudden rush of rage when I recalled laughing with her, sharing jokes, and working together.

"Exactly. Grayson's guys followed Kristoff and overheard the two of them making plans. If you'd gone into my office earlier the way I asked, I would've shown you the photos. The two of them were out on a date more than once."

"That *bitch*. And that *fucking dick*!" I didn't know there were people like them in the real world. There I was, thinking Brandon was the biggest asshole I ever knew. Even he wouldn't go to the lengths Kristoff had.

"The way I saw it, there hasn't been open animosity between us for years. He's been giving me that act he gave us the night you met him. Water under the bridge and all that shit."

"What did you do? I mean, no offense, but really. What was so bad he had to do this?"

I didn't expect a straight answer and wouldn't have been surprised if he offered none at all.

"They weren't even dating," he snickered, shocking me with his openness. "The girl. Rachel, her name was. They worked together in a kitchen. He was obsessed with her. Kept telling me she was the one. They went out once or twice, but she didn't seem interested in anything more. He told me that and wondered what he could do differently to change her mind."

I could have told the loser a woman's mind didn't work that way. We couldn't be coerced, worn down, and even if we could, there wouldn't be anything real behind it. Wearing a woman down wasn't exactly something to be proud of.

"Then we met one night when I caught up with them after my shift," he continued. "I was going to school during the day and working as a line cook at night. I knew right away she wanted me and not him. She practically groped me and laughed it off like she was drunk when I didn't go for it. I'm not trying to be a dick," he added. "That kind of shit has always bored me."

Was that why he didn't fall under Hadley's spell? Interesting. I was wondering since she did everything but lie on her back and throw her legs into the air, but I didn't want to come straight out and ask. It would have been rude, not to mention maybe be a little bitchy.

"Kristoff noticed and freaked out when that happened," he continued. "Right away, he tried to make another move on her. He had to claim what he saw as his property. She wasn't interested and told him off in front of the entire bar. He blamed me, even when I wasn't interested in her. He wouldn't hear it. He couldn't imagine me *not* wanting her. Fucking pathetic." There was a growl in his voice by the time he finished mixed with disdain.

"And that's it? He would go to all this trouble because some girl rejected him?"

"I'm telling you, he was convinced she was 'the one.' " He made finger quotes and rolled his eyes. "They were going to work side by side in the kitchen for the rest of their lives. When I graduated with my business degree, Nonna and my parents helped me pull together the money for the restaurant. I know I'm lucky," he added solemnly. "Not everyone has that opportunity. He took it personally. I heard through mutual acquaintances he decided he was going to outdo me by opening a restaurant of his own."

"But he hasn't because you actually had the passion," I concluded.

"Claudia Granger." There was teasing awe in his voice. "Did I just hear you call me passionate?"

Kicking gently, I retorted, "You really know how to take a compliment and beat it into the ground, don't you?" I had to laugh along with him, breaking the tension in the air after his story ended.

His laughter died all at once, like muting the volume on a radio. "I'm telling you, honest to God, I didn't do a damn thing to antagonize him," he insisted, serious again, gazing at me from the other end of the bed.

"I believe you." He didn't look convinced, leaving me to stare at him in surprise. "I mean it. I believe you." I sensed his concern with my opinion. I saw it in his steady, intense stare. *Why is it so important to him that I believed him?*

"Thank you." A smile tugged the corners of his mouth, almost sheepish. It made him look younger. "Somehow, knowing you believe me makes a difference. I'm no angel, but I'm not an asshole. Not that kind of asshole," he amended when I couldn't hide a smirk.

"Sorry, but you know you can be." I pulled my feet back when he reached out, growling like he was about to tickle them. "And Kristoff is a petty little bitch." Now, I wished I hadn't been so nice to him when he introduced himself. *The dick.* Going to all this trouble over a grudge when the girl wasn't even into him. *What a loser.*

"Just for that, I will not take your feet," he decided.

Rolling my eyes, I replied, "Oh, thank you."

I should have known better.

All at once, he grabbed them, holding my ankles under one arm and tickling the soles until I screamed and squirmed, begging for mercy.

Not that I really wanted him to stop.

Not when it felt this nice and natural.

When was the last time somebody had taken care of me?

It was a question that echoed in the back of my mind long after we decided to call it a night. It wasn't like I was in a hurry to fall asleep since a very big part of me wanted to live in the moment, the small spoon to his much bigger spoon.

How was it that Sebastian Kennedy, of all people, knew exactly what I needed and how I needed it?

15

SEBASTIAN

I wanted to do this about as much as I'd want a root canal.

There was no choice but to sit and play nice in my restaurant dining room, which I had chosen specifically for this meeting. I wanted this asshole on my home turf. This was as close as Kristoff would ever get to one of my restaurants again.

"I don't know why I never came in." He looked around the room, studying everything with those beady rat eyes of his, though he did his best to look casual.

Let him. Let him see everything he wanted to see. It was the last chance he'd get.

"Please. I, of all people, know how busy you must be." *Did I ever.* "I can't even tell you the last time I saw my housekeeper. I'm hardly ever home long enough to give her any work to do."

"Well, I can see why customers have raved about this food for so many years." He dragged a crust of bread through the rich bolognese left on his plate, sopping up every last drop of what had simmered for eight hours. "It's fantastic. So flavorful."

That was about as much ass-kissing as I could take. I hadn't brought him here to remind him what good cooking tasted like, though it was a bonus. As it was, sitting across from him all this time had strained my patience to its limit. "There's something I think we need to discuss. I would like to clear the air once and for all."

It was funny how his eyes darted back and forth before he said anything, like he was looking around, confused as to why I would bring this up in the open among my diners. The restaurant was beginning to empty out after our last seating, with only a few late-comers still lingering over dessert and coffee. "Don't worry, I won't start hurling accusations in front of the public," I assured him with a tight, empty smile I couldn't maintain for long. "But this does need to be said."

I paused before dropping the hammer, savoring his strain. "Enough fucking around. I'm onto you now. I know what you've done."

His Adam's apple bobbed. "Fucking around? I don't understand."

Playing dumb. How original. "In my office, I have a series of documents detailing your involvement with a few issues I've had over these past several months, ever since I announced my expansion. Don't waste my time," I warned when he had the nerve to look stricken, surprised. "I found out who you paid off to schedule that inspection we almost failed with for no reason. I know the names of your contacts in the union. And I'm sure your girlfriend told you I dropped her like a bad habit last week," I concluded.

"Girlfriend?" He blurted out a laugh. "I don't have a girlfriend."

"Fuck buddy, employee you finger every once in a while. I don't care about the specifics. I know you sent her here as a spy." He still had the nerve to sputter, deepening my thirst to put him in his place. "Don't insult my intelligence by denying it. I'm telling you *enough*," I concluded, watching the blank shock that came over him once I went silent. It was like he knew I had him cornered, and there was no point pretending anymore.

Still, he managed to disappoint me. "I admit, I knew Marissa applied for a job after leaving my restaurant, but as for the rest of it—"

"I've given the information to my lawyers," I concluded, finishing what was left of my scotch while he processed this. "They seem to think I have enough to press charges, thanks to the way your pals squealed like stuck pigs at the slightest bit of pressure. I don't think you paid them enough," I added in a whisper, barely fighting off a laugh when his face fell.

He still found the nerve to lift his chin and puff out his chest. "So that's what this is all about? I cannot believe you would make these accusations." Oh, yes. Kristoff Darden's School of Acting. This was the part where he became the wounded party to deflect from the truth of the accusations. I had seen it more times than I cared to remember throughout the days of our friendship, that is, if we were ever really friends. If anything, we were roommates who hung out sometimes. When you're young, you don't understand the difference.

"Consider this a warning," I concluded once it seemed like he had himself under control. "If I find out you're interfering in my business one more time, that's it. The gloves come off. And my lawyers would love to earn their retainer and then some."

When his eyes narrowed, I knew he was dropping the act. "How do I know you're not going to go back on your word?" he asked and added, "If what you say is true."

"You don't even have the balls to admit what you've done," I observed, unsurprised. "You'll have to take my word for it, won't you? Because let me warn you..." I added, leaning in and lowering my voice until it was a stern whisper only he could hear, "... if anything goes wrong from here on out... a bad review, a clogged drain, an act of God, I am holding you accountable, and I will *bury you.* Do we understand each other?"

The word *hatred* was the only one that sufficed in

describing the expression he wore when he stood, his normally tanned skin suspiciously pale. Tossing his napkin onto the table with more force than necessary, scoffed and then shot me a cold glare before walking away without another word.

What was there to say?

Nothing I would want to hear, anyway.

I left the table and entered the kitchen, feeling like a new man, as if a weight had been lifted from my shoulders. It had taken the better part of a week after learning of his treachery to decide how I wanted to deal with him. In the end, it seemed wise to give him a warning rather than stir up a scandal so close to the soft opening next week. At the same time, I didn't want to give him too long a leash. He needed to know I was acutely aware and that I was watching.

"It looked like he was going to puke." Of course, Claudia had watched from the window in the kitchen door, probably standing on her tiptoes to see over the bottom edge. "What did he say?"

"Nothing beyond the empty self-defense I knew I would hear. He gave up the act quickly, though," I concluded. The fact was, I didn't want to talk about him now. Not when those big, shining eyes twinkled up at me. This meant just as much to her as it did to me, and there was something special about that. Something that went beyond the solidarity my friends expressed.

And I wanted to celebrate. "Listen. Everything's

under control around here," I pointed out, noting the cleanup preparations already taking place while the last remaining diners wrapped things up. "There's something I want to show you. Come with me."

"Where?" she asked, removing the latex glove she wore over her right hand in the days after her burn. The doctor I'd insisted she see assured her there was no infection. It was well on its way to healing now, with only a gauze pad on her palm and the high-vis blue Band-Aids on her fingertips to keep her comfortable.

"You'll see." There was nothing I enjoyed as much as teasing her like this, especially when I was feeling hopeful and positive for the first time in forever. The new assistant Felix hired a couple of days after Marissa's dismissal eagerly picked up the slack, learning on the fly as Claudia explained her processes and the rhythm she and Stella had established. After the opening, Naomi would take her place at Home Again, overseeing a trio of bakers, while Claudia split her time between both locations the way I would.

The pieces were all in place.

Nobody could take this from me.

Claudia said her goodbyes first while I waited ten minutes or so before leaving. There was still a need for discretion for her sake. I couldn't have cared less whether the crew knew we had a deeper relationship going, but she felt it important to keep up the charade.

She was gone by the time I pulled out. When I called, she answered immediately, her voice slightly distorted as it echoed through her car. "Where are we going?" she asked.

"Patience, Granger," I urged, chuckling when she growled. "Was that supposed to be menacing?" As usual, she was waiting a few blocks from the restaurant, pulling out behind me when I slowly passed her. Instead of leading the way to my house like I had almost every night since she got burned, I led her down the Strip, grinning while she grumbled.

I almost couldn't believe the day was so close when there had been so many doubts and questions. "I want to thank you," I murmured as I drove, glancing at the rearview mirror to confirm she was still behind me. "A lot of this wouldn't have been possible without you."

"What do you mean by that?"

"We've already talked about it. I needed you to help clean up and refresh my brand, and you did. If my investors hadn't been convinced we were back on the right track, they would've pulled funding. I couldn't do any of this without you now," I concluded. Perhaps being over the phone made it that much easier to admit. "So thank you. I don't take that for granted."

She released a soft breath. "You're welcome, but then you know you sort of saved me too. I went from being engaged to Brandon and prepared to start a new job to shattered and directionless, all because I came home earlier than expected and found a party going on in my bed." Her bitter chuckle practically lowered the temperature. "I needed a job that didn't involve me talking to invisible viewers through a camera. I guess I wanted to prove to myself that I'm not this flash-in-the-pan phenomenon with nothing more to offer. You've given me the chance to try new things and gain steady experience in a professional kitchen rather than jumping from one appearance to another. So thank you too," she concluded. I had to admire her simple honesty in the moments before we reached our destination.

It did my heart good, seeing that only the final touches needed to be made to the landscaping as I pulled into what would be the parking lot of Home Again. "What are we doing here?" she asked, pulling in beside me before I ended the call and stepped out of the car. That gave me the pleasure of watching her follow suit, looking skeptical but curious by the time she joined me.

Sweeping an arm outward, I announced, "Here we are. The last of the equipment was loaded in today, tested, and deemed ready for use. But I wanted you to give it your stamp of approval."

Her mouth fell open, her eyes became wide, and then she squealed and bounced on the balls of her feet like a joyful little girl. "Oh my God! Hurry, hurry, I want to see!" The effect her excitement had on my heart was damn painful. It took so little to make her that happy. How could I do it again?

For now, it was enough to watch her almost skip excitedly up to the front door of the building, which I unlocked with a flourish. "I think you can find the kitchen on your own," I suggested after turning on the lights to guide her way. She took her time, though, admiring the work the crew had put in over the last few days since she had last visited here. While the original Home was conceived as a trip to Nonna's house, complete with black-and-white family photos on the walls, this was meant to bring to mind a trip to Tuscany. There was a more earthy feel to the décor, and the artwork on the walls depicted vineyards and rolling hills, the sort of vistas my grandfather had admired when he was a boy before he made the trip to the States.

I was right behind Claudia when she entered the kitchen and immediately stopped dead in her tracks. "Oh, that is so fucking sexy," she whispered, walking as if in a trance toward the gleaming row of burners which preceded a trio of ovens whose glass doors revealed their pristine interiors.

"Impressed?" I asked, watching her inspect the equipment gently, gingerly, like she was afraid of hurting it.

"Impressed is not the word. Do you understand this is, like, virgin," she explained, and she was dead serious. "We'll be the first people to ever use it. What a treat."

Pure happiness radiated from her face when she turned to me all at once and threw her arms around my waist, squeezing tight. "I love it. I can't wait to get started."

I didn't have time to return her embrace before she pulled her head back, gasping. "Oh, can I try a couple of recipes here? Oh, *please*, I won't ruin anything. But I would like to get a feel for the equipment before it's time to welcome guests, you know?" She was doing her damnedest to legitimize her request, and I couldn't help but laugh indulgently.

"If it means keeping the guests happy." The light in her eyes damn near took my breath away. *What else could I do to make that light always burn?* I was willing to find out. I could hardly believe it, but it was true. Somewhere along the line, her happiness had come to matter a lot to me. And as I stared down at her, I realized she mattered a lot to me.

"What about keeping the boss happy?" she asked, a smile playing over her lips. "What would make you happy right now?"

Interesting. I noted the change in energy between us, the shift in her tone. I would have been the world's biggest jackass if I didn't go with it. There was something fresh and new about being with her. She was unpredictable, which added a layer of excitement and kept me on my toes. It made moments like this so much more rewarding.

As rewarding as the sight of her sinking to her knees. "What about this?" she asked, gazing up at me while running her hands over my thighs. "Would it make you happy if I unzipped these pants and took out what's inside? It's already getting so big."

It was pressing against my zipper, demanding attention. But it was the look in her eyes—wild, sensual, seductive—that made it necessary to lean against the prep table while she worked my belt and unbuttoned my waistband.

"This will be the first time you do this here too," she pointed out, flashing a grin and turning her attention to what awaited her. With my hands gripping the table's edge, I watched, holding my breath while she lowered the zipper. The woman held my life in her hands as she dipped one inside my boxer briefs and slowly withdrew my throbbing dick.

There was nothing like getting head from someone who loved giving it, and it was clear as Claudia extended her tongue and ran it from my base to my tip that she was one of those people. There was no hurrying through it, no forcing herself. She savored my helpless grunts, licking my length again and again until I was sure it would snap if it got much harder.

"Put it in your mouth," I had to demand, aching, dripping, and needing the warmth of her around me. There was nothing I wanted more.

"Whatever you say," she whispered, making me surge again before she guided my head between her waiting lips and made my world explode.

"Fuck..." I sighed, my eyes closing and my knees going weak because she took me deep, not stopping until I hit the back of her throat. Her low, sensual moan left me groaning helplessly in return, the vibrations adding to the heat of the friction from her tongue. It was heaven, nothing less, and I wished it would never end even as my balls ached for release.

I opened my eyes and watched her work, watched my glistening shaft disappear before reappearing, her lips moving up and down my length in a steady rhythm. "That's right," I whispered, stroking her hair and burying my hands in it to guide her progress. "Nice and slow. Take all of it, Granger."

Her deep, throaty moans made my head spin and left me fighting to hold on, to savor every second. This beautiful, talented, infuriating woman was on her knees in front of me, so eager and expertly sucking my cock. *If I'm dreaming, back the fuck up and let me be.*

But it wasn't a dream. Not even the most vivid dream was this good, filled with her moans, the vibrations they caused, the almost unbearable pleasure that ran through me with every stroke of her tongue. There was only so much I could take before desire obliterated everything else.

"Just like that," I grunted, letting instinct take over. I thrust into her greedy mouth, her tongue pressed against my underside and swirling around my head until I plunged deep again. Soft, thick silky hair slid between my fingers as I worked my way in and out, fucking her face.

Our eyes met, and the look I found there was all it

took. The familiar tingle began at the base of my spine and quickly spread, making me grip her head tighter, working my hips faster. "Close... so close..." I whispered, feeding myself to her faster, deeper, realizing in the back of my mind she was fighting to keep up in the final seconds before the thrill of release overtook me and threatened to tear my soul from my body.

"Oh my God!" I filled her mouth, emptying down her throat, sighing in satisfaction when it was finished, and she slowly let me drop from her lips.

"What the hell was that about?" I asked with a breathless chuckle, my head spinning as I leaned against the table for support. "Not that I'm complaining. Send me to the doctor if I ever complain about that."

"My way of saying thank you," she told me with a grin, winking as she stood.

"Well, you've sort of created a problem," I explained, zipping my fly with trembling hands. Her face fell until I explained, "Now, I'm going to have to thank you back. And before you know it, we're just going to be thanking each other back and forth forever."

Had I used the word forever?

Would she take it the wrong way?

She didn't seem to notice, too busy eyeing me. "What can we do about that?" she asked before sinking her teeth into her lip. How was that simple gesture so damn captivating?

"I really think we need to go back to my place and think it over," I decided.

With a sigh, she shrugged. "You're the boss. Whatever you think is best."

"Word to the wise." Taking her hand, I pulled her along with me out of the kitchen. "Be careful saying shit like that because I'll hold you to it." Her playful grin left me wondering if she would mind very much if I did.

16

CLAUDIA

The custard I had created left a bit to be desired.

Hardly the most pressing problem a person ever had, but we were only a few days out from the soft opening, and I wanted everything to be perfect. Sebastian's entire family would be here, including cousins coming from out of town, not to mention all of his friends. He had made a point of having me invite Hadley out too. Until now, she wasn't completely sure how he felt about her, what sort of impression she'd left. Knowing he'd encouraged me to have her out for the opening meant the world to both of us.

The thought made me smile to myself as I prepared yet another custard for the trifle I was determined to nail. All of the elements had to work in perfect harmony, and at this point, there was still a lack of balance that was driving me wild. Not the way Sebastian normally drove me wild, either, though the thought did turn my frustrated scowl into a grin. The nights we'd spent together had come to mean so much to me. More than the sex, which was incredible enough on its own, but I liked the talking, bouncing ideas off each other.

And then, once the conversation was over, we'd have sex again.

Not a bad arrangement.

Soft jazz played on my phone, helping me feel a little less lonely as I worked by myself late into the night. It was the only time I had to practice with things being so busy at the restaurant. There had been so much hubbub and excitement over this opening. The results had to justify the buildup.

Restarting my playlist meant the excuse to reread Sebastian's last text before he went to bed.

Sebastian: *It'll be a little cold and lonely without you —that trifle had better be worth it.*

He wasn't the only one who felt that way, joking or otherwise.

I might have been missing out on the chance to spend a late night having much more fun than this, but the work had its rewards. What a joy it was to use this new equipment. I treated it reverently because that was what it deserved. Like a proud parent, I turned off the gas under the double boiler and moved it to a cold burner before lifting the glass bowl from atop the saucepan where water still simmered. I had gone through countless egg yolks and more vanilla than I wanted to think about, but the flavor wasn't quite there. *What do I need to add?* Almond extract, maybe? That would pair well with the chocolate cake and cherry preserves I would layer it with. Inspired, I went to the pantry to find the extract, whistling to myself as I did.

When was the last time I felt this energized about my work? This hopeful? No, I wasn't revolutionizing anything, but I was having fun. I had the pleasure of watching guests enjoy themselves, too, which was just as important—another thing I had missed out on during my training and time on the show. Sure, I'm *America's Best Baker*, whatever that was worth, but the real pleasure existed in observing others enjoying my work. That was satisfying. It made all the long hours worth it.

I placed plastic wrap over the custard to keep it from forming a skin on top before leaving it in the walk-in to set up, glancing at the clock as I did. Three thirty! *How the hell did that happen?* No wonder I could barely keep my eyes open, not to mention the tightness in my neck and shoulders. At least I was somewhat satisfied with the finished product after going through countless versions that just weren't quite right. I couldn't wait to put it all together once the custard was chilled, and I would have as close an experience as possible to what the guests would enjoy once they got here. I couldn't wait to let Sebastian test it. I hoped he would be happy.

I certainly was.

It was lame, of course. Being this happy, joyful, and wanting to share it with a man who, for all I knew, had no interest in such things. We had a lot of fun, he challenged me the way I challenged him, and we worked well together.

I knew I would have to leave it there. I couldn't get too personal with him. What would happen if things between us went south, which there was no way of guaranteeing they wouldn't? I had a good thing going here. I was proud of my work and looked forward to it every day. Didn't I owe myself? Shouldn't I protect what really mattered?

What the hell was I doing thinking about things like that when I couldn't stop yawning? That was the real problem. I only realized after I'd finished cleaning up that I wasn't sure I could make it home without falling asleep on the road. It occurred to me that I could try to find an Uber, but that would mean leaving my car here and coming back to get it in the morning. That was a big hassle I didn't feel like dealing with later on.

What appealed more to my weary body was the idea of spending some time in Sebastian's new office—bigger and nicer than the other one, for sure. For starters, there was an actual sofa and a desk that didn't look like it had come out of a storage closet. It made me happy for him. He deserved a nice, comfortable office like the one I retreated to after turning off the music and flipping off the kitchen lights.

Being here alone was a little eerie, but what mattered more was closing my eyes after dropping onto the couch, stacking a couple of throw pillows under my head, and kicking off my sneakers. I would take a short nap, just enough to make sure I could get home without wrecking the car. I didn't have to be in early, meaning I hadn't fucked myself over too badly by working practically until morning.

This was the right idea. I couldn't get up now if somebody put a gun to my head. I fell asleep with a smile, looking forward to tomorrow. When was the last time I was able to do that?

It was the alarm that woke me.

I must have been out cold because the sudden high-pitched shriek made me sit up, confused, with no clue what I was supposed to do. *What's happening?*

It only took a moment for the cloud of confusion to clear. When it did, I realized why the deafening alarm had gone off. Smoke was beginning to slip in from under the door.

The kitchen was on fire.

There was only one brief, heart-stopping moment of panic before a sense of calm came over me. I knew what to do, just like I knew giving in to panic would kill me. The alarm would send a call directly to the fire department, but how long would it take them to get here? How big was the fire? Would I have time before it became too much? I couldn't afford to sit around and wait.

Scrambling off the sofa, grabbing my purse as a last-second afterthought, I went to the door and touched the back of my hand to it. *Fuck, that siren was going to crack my skull open.* The door wasn't too warm, giving me hope for what I'd find when I opened it. Just in case, I filled my lungs with all the air they could hold, wrapping the bottom of my shirt around my hand and turning the doorknob.

The smoke was thick, choking me in an instant, making it impossible to see. I lifted my collar over my nose and mouth, but that didn't do much good, leaving me coughing as I sank as low as I could, almost hugging the floor. I wasn't super familiar with the kitchen yet, but I knew which direction to head in, bearing left and crawling for the door leading to the back lot.

No go. Flames licked the door, the heat intense enough to make me crawl backward to get away from it. I couldn't breathe! Every cough was torture, but I couldn't afford to stop moving. *How much longer will it take before the firefighters arrive?*

My eyes were burning with tears running down my face. I turned around, heading toward the dining room this time, while the wall above the stove and oven quickly became consumed by flames. The kitchen, the beautiful kitchen, it was all going up in smoke. It was too late for me to do anything about it. I could only keep crawling, inching along, my lungs burning, every breath agony. I wasn't getting enough air. *Which direc-*

tion should I head? I didn't know anymore. I kept going, forcing myself through it, crawling with my eyes closed when it hurt too much to keep them open.

When I came up against a solid barrier, I ran my hands over it until I found the part that moved when I pushed—the swing door leading to the dining room. I leaned my body against it, forcing it open. The dining room wasn't that smoky, but that didn't mean much when it felt like all the smoke was now in my lungs. I couldn't take a breath or stand on my feet. I could only keep crawling toward the door. The lights from the street beyond the parking lot were barely visible as the smoke quickly filled the space, intensifying, that ear-splitting alarm still shrieking.

I had to get out.

But I couldn't move anymore.

My head was too heavy, and my body weighed a ton.

Sebastian, I'm sorry. I burned down your restaurant.

Lowering myself to the floor, touching my cheek to the hardwood, I closed my eyes.

Suddenly, what was left of my self-preservation broke through my oxygen-deprived brain. *No. I would tell him in person, goddammit.* I was not going to die here. I didn't know if I was wheezing or sobbing or both as I dragged my body toward the door, forcing myself up on my knees to unlock it and almost collapsing from the effort. I leaned against it for a few seconds, hacking painfully before taking hold of the handle and throwing my body against the door to force it open.

The shrieking siren was replaced by another, this one getting louder as a red engine with flashing lights turned off the road and pulled into the lot. I had never seen anything so beautiful in all my life, even through my now cloudy vision.

They were here.

They would help me.

It was a good thing because I couldn't help myself anymore, collapsing on my side beneath the awning bearing the restaurant's name.

17

SEBASTIAN

The automatic doors hadn't even finished sliding shut behind me when my voice cut through the room, commanding attention and wide-eyed stares from every person waiting to be seen. "Granger! Where is Claudia Granger?" I shouted.

Was I being too loud?

Did I give a shit?

I cared about nothing but seeing her since I got the call telling me about the fire and the woman found lying unconscious outside the restaurant. She had told me she was thinking about working in the new kitchen, making everything perfect for the soft opening.

Now, here I was, facing the possibility of losing her along with the new kitchen.

The woman at the triage desk waved me over, holding a finger to her lips as if that would do anything but make me more determined to scream. "Who are you looking for, sir?" she asked because, apparently, I hadn't been loud enough the first time around.

Barely suppressed rage made my voice tremble. "Claudia Granger. There was a fire. She was brought in from the scene."

"Of course. Wait one moment, please, and I will find out—"

"You'll find out now where she is, or I'll go back there on my own. It doesn't matter," I declared, already on my way to the swinging doors leading back to the emergency room bays.

"Sir! We can't let you do that," the woman called out as if I'd asked for permission. A nurse exiting the ER opened the doors with her badge, and I took advantage by sliding past her.

"Claudia Granger!" I shouted, gaining the attention of nurses and orderlies who stopped in their tracks to stare at me as I searched.

"Sir?" A nurse came trotting my way, looking stern. "I can't allow you to run through here, shouting and disturbing the patients. I'm going to have security escort you out."

Instead of tearing her head off, I grunted, "My name is Sebastian Kennedy. It was my restaurant that caught fire." Fuck, I could barely get the words out. "I'm looking for Claudia Granger. I was told they brought her here."

"I see." Her features pitched together in something

closer to sympathy. "I'll take you to her. Don't worry. Smoke inhalation, that's all. She was very lucky."

That was serious enough, but in the grand scheme of things, it was the best I could hope for. There I was, imagining her badly burned. My mind had gone to the worst-case scenario immediately upon getting the call.

What I found upon entering the curtained-off area where Claudia waited on a gurney was still harrowing. Her face was streaked with soot left behind by so much smoke. The odor clung to her, almost choking me the closer I drew. Not that it would have kept me away. Nothing could have.

She breathed slowly, haltingly from the mask placed over her face, pumping the oxygen she desperately needed. A hacking cough left her convulsing. The sound and the sight of it broke through my shock, and I went to her, standing by the gurney, stroking her hair.

Her eyes slowly opened and moved over my face. A strangled cry threatened to tear itself from me. She was alive, looking up at me when I was so sure I would never speak to her again. "Thank God," I whispered, bending to brush my lips against her forehead. "Oh, thank God. You're all right."

I was only able to hear because I was so close. "Define... all right..." She wheezed before coughing again. Even now, she couldn't help but be a smartass. I was never so grateful to hear it.

"You're here, and you're looking up at me, and that's a good place to start."

"But... kitchen... restaurant..." She closed her eyes, wincing like it hurt to speak, which I had no doubt it did.

"You don't have to say anything," I insisted, finding her grimy hand and closing mine around it. "Nothing matters but you being safe."

Though now that I knew she was safe, unburned, and receiving treatment, other thoughts managed to work their way into my overheated mind. Questions. *How? Why?*

"It was me," she rasped, squeezing my hand tight. "Had to be."

She was certain. I was not. I was certain of other things, such as knowing it was now close to eight o'clock on the East Coast. The morning shows would be starting, and soon the word would start to spread. *America's Best Baker* had nearly burned to death in a fire.

"It doesn't matter," I insisted, ignoring the way she groaned. "We'll work it all out. For now, I'll take you home with me once you're cleared for release. In the meantime, I have a few phone calls to make. Word is going to get out. I'll need to help manage the press."

Leaning down, I kissed her forehead again, then made the impulsive move of lifting the oxygen mask to press a quick, fervent kiss against her mouth. "Rest. Breathe. I'll be right back."

In the few minutes since I had found Claudia, I'd

received three phone calls and a half-dozen texts. One of them was from Sienna Black, as it turned out.

Sienna: *Call ASAP. Need to put a story together.*

There wasn't much of a story to be told. "Claudia is fine, unharmed except for smoke inhalation." Saying the words reminded me how much worse this could have gone. "It's too soon to tell the level of damage that was done. I haven't been out there yet, but I'm sure I'll get a full report."

"Please, give her my best wishes," Sienna urged. "I'll take care of things on this end." At least I had that out of the way by the time I ended the call, then immediately sent out a group text so my friends would know I had things under control. They were all early risers, like me, and would surely get word quickly.

Another text, this time to my family so they wouldn't worry.

Sebastian: *Everything okay. Claudia fine. We'll get through this. I'll keep you posted.*

Finally, I called Felix, who, until now, I had only texted on my way out to the car. Never in my life had I gotten a call like that, one of those middle-of-the-night heartstoppers...

"We're sorry, Mr. Kennedy, but there's a fire at your new restaurant. Crews are there now, fighting the blaze. A woman was taken from the scene. She managed to get herself out. She had her purse with her. It's Claudia Granger."

Of course, she had managed to get herself out. She

wasn't a quitter. My heart swelled with pride, and it was the reminder of how brave she must have been that stiffened my spine and confirmed my resolve by the time Felix answered, sounding groggy.

"I hate to wake you up this way…" I told him, "… but I need you to head out to the new location."

Drawing a breath, I closed my eyes and leaned against the wall to my back. Reality was beginning to seep in now that adrenaline was wearing off. There was no hope of making our opening this close to the scheduled date. "It's looking like everything went up in smoke."

And I had a sick, sinking feeling I knew who was behind it.

With that in mind, I made eye contact with one of the cops lingering by the ambulance bay after noticing the way he kept glancing toward me. "Sebastian Kennedy," I said as I approached. "It was my restaurant that burned. What can I do to help with the investigation?"

"You need to keep your head propped up. Remember what the doctor said." Sliding another pillow under her head, I ignored the way she crumbled. After three days of looking after her, I was starting to believe the woman was determined to do the opposite of everything I suggested. "Maybe I should tell you to lie flat on your back, then you would do what you're supposed to do to defy me."

"Very funny. Here I am, laughing," she muttered, doing anything but. Even now, driven half crazy by her stubbornness, I had to chuckle. She was feeling grumpy, which meant she was alive and getting healthier all the time. I'd been instructed to keep an eye on her for three or four days after the fire and look for any signs of deeper issues, pneumonia being the biggest culprit. So far, her biggest problem was her inability to listen to reason. Not even multiple calls from Hadley could convince her.

Hadley wasn't the only one calling, either. More than once, I'd noticed a call coming in from someone she'd named *Cheating Asshole*. It didn't take a genius to know who that meant. *The balls on that cheating asshole.* At least she was smart enough to send him straight to voicemail.

I climbed into bed with her now, prepared to sleep lightly again while I listened to make sure she was breathing well. Anyone witnessing this would tell me I was losing my mind, but they didn't understand. They hadn't seen her lying there, helpless, caked with soot, and unable to breathe without an oxygen mask. They wouldn't understand the guilt of knowing she was like that because of something they had gotten her roped into, even unintentionally. There was no reason for the place to go up in smoke like it had without some sort of interference. I found it hard to believe any other theory while waiting for a full Fire Incident Report from the fire marshal. I'd been assured multiple times they were working as fast as they could, but it wasn't fast enough for me.

Between looking after Claudia and dealing with endless phone calls, requests for interviews, virtual meetings surrounding our plans going forward, I was damn near exhausted. Not so exhausted that my heart didn't warm when Claudia snuggled up against me, fitting her body to mine the way she was so good at doing.

I had almost lost this. Her. I couldn't get the thought out of my head. It kept popping up like a familiar refrain, haunting me. She could have died if she had given up and stopped fighting to get outside. She could have burned, could have succumbed to the smoke. But no, she had fought, and I was holding her. I was holding the woman I was starting to believe I might love.

Sad that it took a fucking fire to make everything so clear. I had never known fear like the fear that had nearly crippled me when I got that call. The entirety of my soul cried out in agony at the idea of losing her forever.

I pressed my lips to the top of her head, and she groaned softly, wiggling against me. "Careful there," I teased, stroking her back. "You don't want to awaken the sleeping giant." It was getting a little tougher every day to be close to her like this and not do anything about it, but she needed to recover. That was the ultimate priority. My dick and his needs could wait.

Or so I told myself before she wiggled again, this time very deliberately brushing against my dick through my underwear.

"Maybe that's what I wanted to do," she whispered, running her hand over my bare abs. "I inhaled a little smoke. I didn't die." She was joking, of course, and she made a good point.

But it wasn't a joke to me. "I just want to take care of you."

"And that is so sweet of you." Her fingers traveled lower, testing my very soul once they brushed against my thickening dick. "But I know what I need. And I need this. Please, don't treat me like I'm going to break," she begged, nuzzling my neck, stroking me through the cotton between us. The T-shirt I'd given her to wear shifted up when she draped her leg over my thigh, exposing creamy skin which my hands ached to touch.

It was enough to break my resolve. Nobody could say I hadn't tried when she lifted her head, her luminous blue eyes staring into mine. I saw the want in them. "Remind me why I bothered getting out of there," she whispered, her mouth seeking mine.

There was no choice but to allow myself to taste what I had stayed away from for days. My skin heated at the connection, the reclaiming of what I craved. Each kiss led to another, my tongue traveling over her lips, delving inside, tantalizing us while inching the shirt farther over her thigh. Her skimpy thong might as well have not existed. I toyed with it, my fingers dancing over the lace that was already moistening over her mound. She was so ready, so willing.

My cock twitched under her hand. She moaned and tugged at my waistband to slide a hand beneath it. I gasped, my body going stiff at the sudden contact. Incredible, electric, something I could have lost. Her fingers wrapped around me, using my precum to move over my shaft. It was paradise, mind-blowing, and I let myself sink into the pleasure while working my fingers under her thong and delving through her swollen folds. Fuck, she was wet, hot, moving her hips against my fingers.

By the time I reached behind me into the nightstand for a condom, she was in a hurry, sitting up to pull the T-shirt over her head and lying back to remove her thong. "No, just like that," I told her before she could roll onto her back. She stayed on her side, facing me, so I could drape her thigh over my hip and line up with her.

Her sharp gasp rang out in my ear once I entered her, and the sound softened to a moan as I slid deep. *Tight, so tight*, determined to make me come. Instinct compelled me to take her hard, fast, to claim her until she screamed my name.

Instead, I moved so slowly, soaking in every bit of her, every inch of me moving inside her. I had to make it last, to memorize every moment, every sound she made, every tender sigh.

How was she so soft? My hand glided over her, sliding down her side, over her hip, then over the leg she draped over mine. I pulled it higher, spreading her wider, sinking in deeper than before.

Her eyes closed, her mouth open in a silent gasp. Her breath fanned across my face, her lips close enough to brush my own. The beating of her heart reverberated against my chest, matching my rhythm. So slowly I could make this last a lifetime if I tried.

"You feel so good inside me," she whimpered, her eyes still closed, her brow furrowed in concentration. It was like she wanted it to last, too, as if she wanted to live fully in every moment. What was it like, having come so close to dying and feeling so alive now? The arm around her back tightened, pulling her tight against my chest. I was afraid to hurt her but unable to resist the need to keep her close. Protected. Safe with me. It wasn't enough to be inside her, to feel her body come alive because of mine. I needed all of her, here and now and always.

I caught her mouth and lips, letting her sighs guide my strokes. She was slick, hot, tightening a little all the time. The soft gasp that sounded when I stroked the curve of her ass cheeks intrigued me, made me do it again, experimenting, toying with her. Giving her all the pleasure she was capable of. Filling her with it the way I filled her with my cock. It was all

I wanted to do, but it was not enough. Nothing ever would be.

"Sebastian," she whispered, her lips traveling down my jaw, over my neck, my shoulder. Her fingers curved into claws that raked my back even as she kissed me tenderly, deeply. I wanted to be lost in her, never to find my way out.

Soon there was nothing but our shuddering breaths, faster all the time. She was getting close, and so was I with every stroke. Her leg clamped tight around me, drawing me deeper, her hips moving with mine.

We were in this together.

And we came together, clutching each other tightly, giving ourselves over to whatever magic we created.

I was here to hold her through it all, and that's what I did I held her throughout the night, long after the rush of heat had passed, listening to her breathing until I was satisfied she was safe.

Only then could I sleep.

"What I don't understand is why you need to go in to work at all?" I was fighting a losing battle, and I knew it as we faced off from opposite sides of the bed the morning after we had sex or made love or whatever the fuck it was we'd done. I couldn't wrap my head around it twelve hours later.

"Because you're already going in to handle things, and I'm tired of lying around." She stomped a foot to punctuate her point. When I sighed in exasperation, she did the same. "I'm serious. Please, don't ask me to hang out here while you go in without me. I appreciate you taking care of me like this, but forcing me to stay locked up isn't helping."

What could I do? She was a grown woman capable of making her own decisions, no matter whether I agreed or not. "If it's that important to you, fine. But I don't want you to overdo it," I added, shaking my head when her mouth fell open, preparing to protest. "That's a hard boundary. If you're tired or winded, you sit down and rest. Otherwise, you oversee things. You don't spend all that time on your feet."

"You didn't seem to care so much about me being tired and winded last night," she reminded me.

"You were the one lying down..." I shot back, buckling my belt with a smirk. "I did all the heavy lifting." She couldn't argue with that, and I couldn't argue with her dedication.

Within the hour, we were parked behind the kitchen as usual, with me resisting the impulse to help Claudia out of her car. She would hate it if I tried the withering look she'd given me when I suggested driving her was bad enough. Settling to wait for her by the back door, I held it open and followed her inside.

"Oh! Claudia!" Stella forgot whatever she was in the middle of doing, rushing over with her arms outstretched. "We were so worried when we heard. Oh my God!"

"I checked in on her and tried to convince her to take it easy," I announced, hands lifted in surrender in case anyone thought to blame me. "She wouldn't listen."

"Hey, Chef." Lucas draped an arm around her shoulders when Stella finally released her. His curious glance my way left me reflecting on the silent communication people could develop when they'd worked together for as long as we had. His gaze darted to her, then back to me, an eyebrow arching. I shrugged, offering a slight nod.

He considered it for a few moments, then shrugged the way I had, a slight smile lifting the corners of his mouth—*message received and accepted.* "Good to see you," he told her once he'd processed the news. "Are you sure you're okay to be here?"

"I am absolutely fine." However, I heard the weakness in her voice, her shallow breathing. It was one thing to feel fine when all she did was sit up in bed all day, but now she was on her feet. She did her best to keep her chin up, though. "Thank you."

Lucas turned his attention my way, concern knitting his brows together. "How's it looking over there? I drove past... it was pretty grim."

My mood darkened, rage clouding my brain. "Not great. The fire marshal is supposed to get back to me any time now."

"It just seems like after everything else that already happened..." I could practically see inside his skull, and it was clear we were thinking along the same lines.

"I probably left something on," Claudia insisted, full of sadness and self-reproach. "It was so late. I was moving on autopilot. I could have left a burner on."

"Let's wait and see before we start blaming anyone, including ourselves," I advised. I needed to take my own advice since, in my mind, Kristoff was already in prison for arson. He wouldn't be stupid enough to leave evidence behind, though. Would he?

The sense of living in limbo was close to driving me crazy by the time service began. Of course, our guests wanted to hear about Claudia, concerned over her well-being after hearing about her on the news. Though I didn't love the idea, she decided to pop her head out from the kitchen to greet people a few times during the course of the evening, like she was proving she was alive and well.

Seeing their reactions warmed my heart, realizing how genuinely relieved they were to find her in good shape. When I reflected on my attitude the first couple of weeks Claudia was with me, how I'd disparaged these people along with her for being locked in this strange fame game, I was ashamed of myself. They truly seemed to care.

I made sure she sat and rested between times, threatening to tie her to the chair in my office more than once. "I heard you out there, and you sounded weak," I told her at one point late in the evening, checking my phone for only the hundredth time, hoping for a message pointing me toward the fire's origin.

Her face screwed up like she was ready for battle, but one of the servers called out, stopping her. "Claudia? There's somebody out here who wants to see you."

We exchanged a look.

"Who is it?" she asked while she rubbed a hand over her face, exhausted. No amount of pretending would convince me otherwise.

"He wouldn't say. He just said he was a friend who needed to see you."

A male friend? I arched an eyebrow, jealousy tightening my chest. She only shrugged. "I don't have any guy friends. I really don't have any friends out here at all," she insisted.

"Probably some asshole reporter thinking he can lure you into making an appearance," I decided. "I'll get rid of him."

"No, let me," she insisted as she stood with a weary sigh. "I can't have you do all my fighting for me."

I admired her strength, but there was something she didn't understand—that was all I wanted to do. I would be her warrior because I now knew for sure how brave she was. How hard she fought to make it out of the kitchen. The least I could do was ease some of her challenges by taking some of the burden off her shoulders.

Especially since I was convinced Kristoff set the fire as a final *fuck you.*

I followed at a slight distance, giving her space. She opened the door to the dining room, her head swiveling as she took in the tables, then froze at the side of a tall, contrite-looking man who stood at the bar.

I didn't need to ask who he was. I knew it the moment I identified the look on his face like *she was his.*

Her single, whispered word confirmed what I'd suspected. "Brandon."

18

CLAUDIA

No fucking way.

He was *not* standing in front of me, having the nerve to look slightly tearful as he approached. “I had to come out,” Brandon murmured while I fought the impulse to shudder at the sound of his voice. There had been a time when I loved the sound of it. When I loved him.

But I didn’t anymore. I now had someone who genuinely cared about me in a way Brandon never could.

“You didn’t bother telling me you were coming,” I muttered, my teeth clenched in a fake smile. Was this really happening? Was I playing nice in front of customers?

“As soon as I heard, I booked the flight, and I’ve been hanging around every night hoping to see you here. You can’t hold it against me,” he insisted in a soft voice. No doubt, many people had asked about me in the days since the fire. I had no idea he was one of them, or I might not have come here.

"Is there someplace we can go? Or would you like to sit down here?" he asked, gesturing toward the stool he had taken at the bar. It was the only way he'd been able to walk in without a reservation.

No. Not here. This asshole did not *belong here.* "Why don't we go outside?" I suggested. "Come with me."

It meant turning around to find Sebastian glaring at Brandon over my shoulder. "Everything will be fine," I told him in a soft voice that I hoped wouldn't betray my nerves. "I don't want to cause a scene in here."

It was obvious he was ready to explode—jaw tight, nostrils flared, his chest rising and falling fast. "It'll be fine," I whispered again. Was I trying to convince him or myself? I didn't know the answer, settling on motioning for Brandon to follow me through the kitchen once Sebastian finally stepped aside and let us pass. I didn't make eye contact with anyone in there, going straight for the back door. The sooner I got this over with, the better.

Once we were outside, I immediately took a seat on one of the overturned milk crates by the door. I was winded, and a lot of it probably had to do with the way my pulse raced uncomfortably at Brandon's surprise appearance. How had his presence ever given me anything but a stomach ache? Oh, right, I used to believe he was actually a decent person who cared about me. Trustworthy. Honest.

"You shouldn't have come out," I told him once the door was closed and we were alone. "I really don't have anything to say to you."

How could he look so surprised? "Even now?" he asked, laughing like I told a joke. His chestnut curls gleamed under the light over the door, reminding me how I used to love running my fingers through them. I was a different person then.

"What, did you think a near-death experience would make me rethink my mistakes?" I asked, understanding that was exactly what he thought would happen when he winced. "I didn't make a mistake. That was you as soon as you decided to bring my so-called friend back to my bedroom so you could screw her."

Those dark, puppy dog eyes shone. I hated them now. "That was a mistake. Are you going to make me pay for it for the rest of my life?"

"No, Brandon, because I don't care about the rest of *your life*." I closed my eyes, taking a couple of deep breaths. "This is too much. Thanks for coming all this way, but you didn't need to."

"I can't believe you would be like this. I came out here to beg you to come home with me, where you belong."

If I were capable of it, I would have laughed. Instead, I shook my head, exhausted by the situation and him. It was like I had lived all those years in the dark. Years of loving him, standing by him, believing him when he told me we were forever. The lights were on now, and I saw everything. There was no going back to fix the past, but I could at least make sure not to make the same mistakes.

"I do not belong with you, for one thing," I replied, disdainful. "And for another thing, I wouldn't have come out here if it weren't for you, so stop acting like you had no part in it. This is my home now." That was true, and it startled me a little. Life had a way of forcing my hand, making me face the things I had missed.

"Ridiculous!" he hissed, waving a hand toward the kitchen behind me. "We both know you're going nowhere out here. I've been reading the stuff they're writing online about you and this Sebastian dick working together. Remember the dreams you had? Your Michelin Star? Whatever happened to that? Did you completely give up on yourself?"

He knew how to hit where it hurt. "That is *none* of your business."

"And there's my answer." The bastard had the nerve to sound disapproving. "You gave up. I'm disappointed in you."

"Remind me what gives you the idea I care about your opinion."

"Fine. You don't care about my opinion? What about everybody else back in New York?" Pausing, he folded his arms over his polo shirt, a smug grin touching the corners of his mouth. "Including Bailey Ryan."

He had a way of shocking me, that was for sure. Hers was the last name I expected to hear, a chef I had worked with short-term before the competition to bone up on some of my skills. "What about her?" I asked, affecting a careless attitude when what I felt was anything but.

"I had dinner at her restaurant last weekend," he explained, narrowing his eyes. Studying me, knowing what my reaction would probably be. "She asked about you, saying something about how she wished you were still in town because she's in need of a new pastry chef and thought of you right away."

"You're lying." There was no way. The woman was a legend before she turned forty, boasting a wall full of awards, along with a Michelin Star, which she'd been awarded two years earlier.

"Am I? Why don't you give her a call and find out? She told me she lost your number, but if I could get in touch with you, I should pass on the message. You know the job won't be open for long," he concluded, wearing a familiar smirk that told me he thought he won.

A Michelin Star. Actually working with someone who wanted to innovate. Somebody who wouldn't hold me back but would encourage me to grow. Everything I always wanted back in my hometown. No more desert air, no more being so far away from Hadley and the friends I missed in New York.

No Sebastian.

My stomach dropped as it had when I dangled over the edge of The Strat. We had something here, the two of us, even if the future of Home Again was in jeopardy. In the end, everything would be all right. I was sure of it. I believed in him.

That was what made my decision, knowing I believed in him. He would find a way through this, and I wanted to go along for the ride.

"I will get in touch with Bailey," I decided, standing slowly, careful not to make any quick moves that might leave me feeling dizzy. "Thank you for passing on the message."

"What are you going to tell her?"

"It's none of your business. Not anymore."

"She's not going to wait forever," he snapped. "This is a limited-time offer, and you are not the only pastry chef in the world."

"I realize that, but thank you for the reminder." He had reminded me of so many other things too—*how he was never right for me*. I had only ever tried to convince myself he was, determined to prove Hadley and anyone else wrong for doubting him, my stubborn pride biting me in the ass.

I would not let that happen again. He was not going to lure me back by reminding me of my dreams. He didn't know the first thing about them anymore, just like he'd never known how to really support me. I had already wasted enough of my life giving a shit what he thought. "Now, go. I didn't invite you, and I've seen enough of you to last me the rest of my life."

He hesitated like he was waiting for me to change my mind. When I didn't, his arms dropped to his sides, fists clenched.

I looked at them, then back into his eyes. "Is your hearing going?" I asked. "Please leave. *Now.*"

Rather than follow him back through the kitchen, I sat down again, trembling, knowing I made the right choice. He was my past, and the past was over. The fire had made so many things clear, burning away everything that wasn't necessary.

One of my last thoughts before I figured it was *the end* was of *Sebastian*. The reason I started moving again? *Sebastian.* His appearance at my bedside while I laid there half conscious, scared, and suffering was the same as sunshine breaking through dark storm clouds, lighting up everything around me. My physical condition hadn't changed, but inside, I was healed. He knew I needed him, and he came running.

I was pretty sure I was in love with him, and the idea didn't scare me. Not anymore. I was ready to admit what I wanted, and it was a hell of a lot more than a Michelin Star.

The door opened, and I prepared myself to tell Brandon to fuck off since he had clearly not gotten the hint. But it wasn't him. It was the man who made my heart skip a beat just by existing. A man who stepped outside wearing a scowl that could only mean trouble.

"I hope he didn't say anything stupid," I whispered, touching the back of my head against the wall and closing my eyes with a sigh. "And I'm sorry he showed up like that."

He didn't say anything at first. It took a moment or two for dread to begin growing in my gut. "What happened?" I asked, opening my eyes again, following his progress as he paced.

"Tell me the truth." It was a grunt, his mouth barely moving. "Am I holding you back?"

"Excuse me? Where did that come from?"

"Just tell me. Because you sure as hell sounded different when he mentioned that Bailey woman wanting you to work for her."

"Bailey?" I asked before it all came together. *Of course. How stupid could I be?* I looked up at the camera over the door. Nobody told me the thing picked up sound too. "You had no right to eavesdrop," I said, but I wasn't angry. I was disappointed.

He scoffed, giving me a dirty look. "What, you thought I would send you out here with that dickhead and not be concerned?"

"Don't make this a story about how you were so concerned about me, please." I was too tired for this, overwhelmed, and still shaken up. My nerves were frayed, and my emotions were dangerously close to the surface. "I don't think I have it in me to do this right now."

"Are you going? Tell me now and get it over with because it sure as hell seemed like you wanted to."

I want to stay with you.

I only want to be with you.

The words raced to the tip of my tongue, eager to be voices, but something held me back. Probably the fact that he looked at me like I was the enemy without ever asking how I felt. Did he think to check in and see if I was okay after such a surprise? Did he bother asking what I thought about Bailey's suggestion? No. He came out with accusations.

"I was surprised," I insisted, cringing when he scoffed. "What the hell is wrong with you? Why are you turning on me like this? What! Am I supposed to control who wants me to work for them? Are you that insecure?"

"Excuse me?" Folding his arms, he cocked his head back in disbelief. "Who the hell are you talking to?"

"The man in front of me who never thought to stop for five seconds to see what I actually wanted."

"Give me a break. One of the first things you told me was you wanted that damn star. This asshole comes to town, dangles it in front of you, and you start asking all kinds of questions. Don't fucking lie to me," he warned, baring his teeth. "This restaurant is not a pitstop, and I'm not a stepping stone. Either you're with me, or you're not. Make up your mind right *now*."

"I can't believe you're acting this way, I..." I what? What was I going to say? I was literally asking myself whether or not I was in love with him moments before he came out here and pulled this bullshit act.

"You can't believe I'm acting this way?" Throwing his hands in the air, he barked out a laugh that bounced against the brick wall at my back. "I've lost a massive investment overnight, literally, up in smoke. And now I find out I'm about to lose you because if I wasn't, why the hell didn't you tell him no? You didn't shut down the idea, did you?"

Tell him now. Tell him you don't want to go.

No, dammit.

He doesn't get to dictate how I express myself or when.

"I'm not allowed to think about it?"

His face darkened along with his eyes. "You wouldn't need to think it over if you wanted to stay with me, *dammit.* You know what? Go ahead," he concluded, throwing his hands in the air again. "Go back to New York, which is where I know you wanted to be all along. Work with somebody who's gonna help you achieve your pointless dream. I hope you remember I told you so when you realize how empty and meaningless it really is."

"How *dare* you? I am so sorry my dreams aren't all as wholesome and family-oriented as yours," I muttered, seeing him through new eyes the way I saw Brandon. What the hell was wrong with me? Why was I so ready to ignore the red flags in every man I knew?

"And I'm sorry things have fallen apart with the restaurant. In case you forgot, I was there when it happened. And until Brandon showed up here, you couldn't stop hovering over me. Is it because you actually cared or because you're afraid somebody set the place on fire, and it would've been your fault if I died?"

Yes. That was exactly why. I saw it in the widening of his eyes, the sharp exhale like something hit him. He didn't know I'd overheard a few of his hushed conversations over the past few days, wondering if the fire was intentionally set.

There was no taking it back. Right now, I wasn't sure I wanted to. One long, painful moment after another passed between us, and then he snarled. "You know what? Go," he decided. "I'll take care of your hospital bill and anything else you need, but you are free to go home and resume your life. Thanks for taking a little time to mingle with the common folk on your way to the top."

This couldn't be happening.

I had to be imagining it.

Something that started off so promising turned to shit in the blink of an eye?

Was it me? Was I the problem? Had I driven him away?

When would I stop blaming myself?

He never gave me a chance.

"Thanks for the opportunity," I whispered, tears filling my eyes. I blinked them back, furious, shattered.

Waiting for him to apologize. Wishing he would. Knowing anything I said now would be tainted by the accusation I'd just hurled at him. I had wanted to hurt him the way he was hurting me.

His jaw twitched, and for a brief moment, his rigid posture softened. Then he murmured, "My pleasure." And that was it. Not even twenty-four hours after we made love in his bed, he left me sitting alone on a milk crate behind the kitchen, where I was only able to keep from sobbing when I reminded myself he would be able to see through the camera.

I managed to wait until I was behind the wheel before the tears began to fall.

19

SEBASTIAN

"This sort of thing happens all the time, unfortunately." Aiden sighed unhappily, giving me a sympathetic look. "Everything seems fine until it's not."

I stared at the fire chief's final analysis of last week's fire. The cause—faulty wiring in the new walk-in. The sort of thing the manufacturer would be held accountable for. It wasn't Kristoff, after all.

It occurred to me that I wanted it to be, and was disappointed after reviewing the report. If Kristoff had been behind the fire, there might be something I could control. I could stop him, send him to prison for the rest of his life for nearly killing Claudia, among many other things.

Instead, I'd only been reminded of how unpredictable life was. There were certain things that could not be controlled. Fate could be a fickle bitch.

“Look at it this way,” Vaughn offered. “I know you. You had everything insured to the hilt, right?”

“Of course.” I didn’t mean to sound dismissive. Naturally, it was important that we settle the cause of the fire, and I recoup my investment.

“Do you know how long it will take before all the damage is cleaned up?” Jackson asked, polishing off his drink.

“Well, they can finally get started now since there’s no longer an investigation pending.” There was an uneasiness churning in me, and I couldn’t hide it. I didn’t have the strength. Frankly, I didn’t care, either. “I don’t know if I want to.”

“What?” Aiden burst out laughing, but the sound died when he realized I wasn’t joking.

“What are you talking about?” Grayson asked. “You’re not giving up. That’s not you.”

“I’m not giving up,” I insisted, looking around the table. We had met at one of Vaughn’s lounges tonight on the first floor of his casino, but I was anything but laid-back the way his other guests seemed to be on a Friday night. Suddenly, my suit was too tight, along with my skin. I wanted to burst out of it.

“Because of her?” Vaughn asked. There was that knowing tone in his voice again. He was the expert all because he was married now.

“She has a name,” I reminded him.

“Claudia,” he murmured. “Is she why?”

"It's not as simple as that." Nothing was simple. It had only been a few days since she left. I didn't know if she was still in town, if she had flown to New York, or if she was in Peru. Regardless, it didn't matter.

"There are other pastry chefs in the world," Jackson reminded me. Because as far as they knew, that was all she was—an employee of mine with whom I'd had a falling out.

"Yeah, you can open a second restaurant with another baker," Grayson agreed.

It was Vaughn who merely gazed at me from across the table, his drink in his hand, a gleam in his eye. "But she's more than that, isn't she?" he asked, raising the glass to his lips. It did nothing to hide a faint smirk.

"Wait. What?" Aiden's head snapped around, his eyes getting wide. "Since when? When the fuck were you going to tell us?"

"I wasn't aware I had to check in with you guys on things like this. Should we stay up late and do each other's nails too?" I countered. "Anyway, it doesn't matter. It's over. She's going back to New York to work for some hotshot chef out there so she could finally get what she wanted."

"And you know that how?" Vaughn was not willing to let this go, and I was about to walk away if he didn't stop pushing me.

"It's a simple question," Grayson pointed out when all I could do was glare.

There was nothing to do but come clean. "That asshole ex of hers came around, and I heard them talking about it, and she practically jumped at the idea."

"So she said yes," Aiden concluded. "Was it even his job to offer her?"

"You're not getting it." I looked around the table and found four blank expressions. "She didn't say no, *dammit*. She didn't tell him she had something here that she wanted to hold onto. What am I supposed to make of that?"

"Did you try asking her what she wanted?" Vaughn asked. When I glared at him, he wouldn't back down. "Or did you assume what she wanted?"

"Oh, that's a bad one," Aiden said, clicking his tongue and shaking his head. "Women don't like it when you assume shit."

"Yeah? What, did you read that on a bathroom stall?" Jackson snorted.

"I know I did the right thing, and that's all I need to know. All right? Let's drop it." I had a feeling my words fell on deaf ears.

"Listen. I'm only going to say this once, and I'm going to let it go." Setting the glass down, Vaughn leaned in. "If you want her to stay, you should tell her that. Don't let this go without at least clearing the air. For all you know, she could still be in town, wishing there was a way through this. Don't be an asshole," he warned. "You'll regret it. If she matters to you, clear the air so you can at least say you did everything you could to make it work."

Motherfucker.

I never asked what she wanted.

Looking back, I couldn't believe my stupidity. I was hurt, wounded, so close to telling her how much she meant to me before that smirking asshole showed up and brought all of my deepest fears to the surface. The fear that she would decide staying with me wasn't enough. Working with me, being with *me*. That her ambition could never be fulfilled with me. That she would decide she had made a mistake. That I had held her back. I couldn't have lived with that, so I decided to tank us before she could. And look where it got me—miserable, directionless, unable to think about the next steps when I was stuck on *her*.

"I've got to go," I decided, bolting back the rest of my drink, my phone in hand, before I left the table.

"Thank God," Aiden muttered. "You're about as fun as watching paint dry when you're feeling sorry for yourself."

"Fuck you," I fired back, and their laughter ran out behind me as I headed for the door.

No big surprise, Claudia sending my call to voicemail. I tried a second time on my way to the car. *What to do?* Track her down at her apartment? I had never been there, but I still had the address on file.

On second thought, I took a chance, knowing it might save me time. I could only hope she would answer, that she hadn't blocked my number after our disastrous date.

She hadn't. "Make it quick," Hadley whispered while I slid behind the wheel. "I'm hiding in the bathroom."

A strange way to begin a conversation, but I put it all together quickly enough. "She's there, isn't she?"

"No, I enjoy hiding in the bathroom," she whispered. "I shouldn't even be talking to you. She would skin me alive."

"I made a mistake."

"No shit, Sherlock."

Funny. I liked her a lot more this way when she wasn't trying to awkwardly seduce me. "What do I do? I'm serious," I insisted when she scoffed. What was the point of pride? The girl had damn near thrown up on me. "I fucked up. I need to make it up to her. I want us to be a team. I lashed out... acted before I thought. And I see now what a terrible mistake that was. I just want her to come back. If that's what she wants."

A few moments passed when all I heard was her breathing. "She didn't want to leave in the first place," she muttered. "God, I am being such a bad friend right now, but it's true. She wanted to stay with you, but you never gave her a chance to explain."

"I know." I touched my head to the seat behind it, closing my eyes as a sense of regret bordering on grief settled over me like a shroud. I had caused all of this by forcing her hand. There was no one to blame but myself. "Did she take the new job?"

"She's been in limbo since she got here. Listen, she can work anywhere she wants." Fierce pride rang out in her voice. "That's not the point. She left New York mostly to get far away from Brandon and make a new start. She came back because she has nobody out there now that you fucked everything up. Your line of work doesn't exactly allow a person to develop a social life."

"I know that."

"So I'm all she's got. I don't know whether she plans on staying or if she's only here to lick her wounds," she concluded, softer now. Concerned.

"What do I do?" I asked, pride be damned. "How do I make this right?"

Snorting, she asked, "Honestly? You want to make it right? Or is this all about getting back what you think belongs to you?"

Brutal but fair. I liked her more. She was protective of somebody we both loved. "I want to make it right."

"At this point, nothing short of showing up in person and getting on your knees would do."

Of all times for one of my sister's favorite sayings to come to mind. I had rolled my eyes at it more times than I could count, but it was the only thing that fit now. "Say less."

She wanted somebody on their knees? I could do that.

I had no choice because I needed her.

When the cab rolled up in front of Hadley's apartment building, it was five in the morning Manhattan time. People were already out and about, heading to the gym or work, or walking their dogs. The city was truly a whole other world.

Hadley had assured me Claudia would be up. "She's still on Vegas time," she told me when I confirmed my plans to charter a private jet and fly out. "I swear, she haunts this apartment all night long. I love her, but you're costing me sleep," she concluded. I would have to find a way to pay her back, just as I would have to pay her back for colluding with me.

At the moment, nothing mattered as much as getting the hell out of the cab and upstairs after spending hours ready to burst out of my skin with desperation. Hadley had told the front desk staff that I would be arriving. I appreciated the fact that I had to show ID before they would let me onto the elevator, which took me up to the sixth floor.

As per my instructions, I knocked softly on the door. My pulse was pounding, my palms sweating. It all hinged on this—getting her to listen to me rather than shut me out.

The knob turned, the door swung open, revealing a small apartment with a terrific view through the windows opposite where I stood.

It was the view of Claudia's wide eyes and pale face

that meant more, even when she grimaced. "Motherfucker," she whispered. Her head snapped around so she could glare at Hadley. "You traitor."

"How am I being a traitor by inviting someone to my apartment, where I pay the rent?" she countered, closing her bathrobe around herself.

I stepped into the living room, unable to tear my eyes away from the woman in front of me. I had to make up for lost time, soaking in the sight of her. "Hi," I offered, accepting how she scoffed softly, staring at the floor.

"I'm going back to bed," Hadley announced, yawning loudly. "Try to keep it down out here."

"We are going to talk about this tomorrow," Claudia warned.

"It is tomorrow," Hadley reminded her, blowing a kiss and leaving the room. I waited until her door closed to turn to Claudia, drinking in the sight of her, savoring the smell of the air when she was this near. She changed everything, made it better. No way was I leaving here without her.

"I have nothing to say to you." Her voice shook but not half as hard as her body. *I'd done that. I am the reason she's hurting.* "Do you think this is going to change anything?"

"I'm hoping it will. I fucked up."

"No shit. You hurt me. You treated me like I was nothing, and I'm supposed to want to look at you?" She turned away, walking to the window where the city lights cast her in a silhouette. Every golden strand of hair shone, stirring a yearning deep in my heart. I needed to touch her. I needed her.

"I will never forgive myself."

"Well. That makes everything better, doesn't it?" she spat. "I'm glad I helped you grow or something."

I refused to give up. I had to believe she still felt something. "Would you please hear me out?" I whispered, keenly aware of Hadley being mere feet away. Something told me she hadn't actually gone to sleep. More likely, she was waiting by her door, listening like any best friend would.

"You came all this way," Claudia muttered, lifting a shoulder with her back still turned toward me. "Say what you came to say. But don't expect it to get you anywhere."

I'd had hours to think about this. Now, at the moment, my tongue was thick and clumsy, my thoughts flying in all directions. There was only one thing I could say to sum up everything in my heart. "I love you."

She flinched, wrapping her arms tighter around her trembling, pajama-clad body. If only she would turn around. If I could see her face and she mine, she would know I meant it. "Is that all?" she whispered.

"What else is there? I was wrong. I was stupid. I didn't give you a chance, and it was the biggest… worst mistake I've ever made. You deserve better than that. And I am so desperately sorry."

She took a deep breath, her shoulders rising and falling. "I accept that. I accept your apology. I said things I shouldn't have said too. It was mean. I wasn't thinking about anything but wanting to get back at you because you..." Something suspiciously close to a strangled sob burst out of her. "You broke my heart. You wouldn't give me a chance to tell you I never wanted to leave. I knew it for sure that night. Everything was so clear. I've never had anything with anyone like I had with you. I never felt so alive. Connected."

Forcing a shaky breath, she concluded, "And then, after everything we shared, you turned around and shut the door in my face all because you wouldn't bother to ask what I was thinking."

The truth of her words reverberated in me. I deserved all of it and more. "I don't know what to say except to tell you I'm a hopeless asshole. I was too proud to admit the idea of losing you was unthinkable."

When she began to turn toward me, my heart almost burst out of my chest. If she would look at me, it meant she cared. I hadn't lost her. There was still something inside her that wanted me. "How could you hurt me like that? That's what I don't understand."

"I'll be damned if I know." I held my head in my hands like that would do anything to keep my skull from splitting open as I fought to express everything. "I swear, I will do everything in my power, every day for the rest of my life, to make it up to you. I only need you to give me the chance."

"What about work? You realize the Michelin Star doesn't mean as much to me as it used to, or you would if you had given me the chance to tell you," she added.

"I don't want you to give up on that dream or on any dream that fulfills you. Whatever you want, I want. If it makes you happy, it makes me happy." She scoffed, turning away, shaking her head. "Claudia, the night of the fire, when I thought I lost you, everything became crystal clear. None of this matters without you. I don't want any of it if I can't have you beside me... every day, working together toward *our* vision. Yours and mine. That's all I want, but I need you."

The profound truth behind those words hit me like a truck. I couldn't believe this was happening, that I was sinking to my knees like some lovesick asshole. "I need you," I whispered, my entire heart in the words. "I need you like I need air. These days without you... nothing makes sense. Nothing matters. You brought the missing ingredient to my life, and I can't go without it now."

She ran a hand over her eyes, sniffling. "Missing ingredient? Come on. That's a little corny, don't you think?" There was laughter in her words, gentleness. The sharp edges were smoothed out.

"Since when does that matter when you're in love? What, you think I hop on a private jet every other day and fly across the country for fun? Do you think I get on my knees for anyone but you?"

She was crumbling. I felt it. I saw it. Still, she held herself back. "How do I know it won't happen again?"

"You know it won't happen again because I don't make the same mistakes twice. That much I can promise you with all my heart. I know now the misery of being without you, and I will not go back to that. You can't make me," I insisted.

"So you swear to me." She took one step closer, then another. "You will *not* do this again."

My heart lodged itself in my throat. "I swear on everything I have. Everything I am or will ever be, I will *not* do that again. I will always listen to you."

She chewed her lip, then released a shaky breath while I held mine. "You drive a hard bargain, Sebastian. But I guess I don't want to live without you, either."

Then she chuckled, shrugging. "I'm not as eloquent as you, I guess."

Who needed eloquence when I had her? When I could stand and gather her in my arms, holding her close to me, shaking with relief. She was *mine*. She would always be *mine*. "I love you," I whispered, kissing her forehead, nose, and cheeks before landing on her upturned mouth.

Yes, this was what I needed.

This was what I had missed so badly.

Sharing breath with her, feeling her heartbeat against mine, holding the entire world in my arms.

This was all that mattered. Everything else would sort itself out as long as I had this to come back to.

"I love you," she whispered once I let her up for air. Tears shone in her eyes, but she smiled brilliantly. "You're an idiot, and you drive me crazy, but I fucking love you."

Running my thumbs over her cheeks to catch her tears, I asked, "Who says you're not eloquent?"

20

CLAUDIA

Four Months Later

"This is it." My nerves were shredded, my heart pounding like I was about to go up to the top of The Strat and dangle off the edge. "Are you ready?"

All it took was the touch of Sebastian's hand against my back to spread calm through me. Slowly, a bit at a time, but eventually, I began to relax and loosen up. There wasn't a weight crushing my chest anymore. "I'm ready," he whispered, kissing my head. "There is nothing to be nervous about. Everything is perfect."

He was right. Everything was perfect. Even though things hadn't gone the way we originally planned, somehow, the outcome had turned out better than we could've imagined. Once Sebastian decided not to rebuild what had burned, his investors decided to pack their bags and head for greener pastures.

Yet his friends had stepped up, picked up the slack, and made it possible to do what he realized he should have done in the first place—expand the current location, blend both concepts into one that would balance both the traditions and comforts of home and the freshness and simplicity of authentic Italian cuisine, which could be at times quite different from what people imagined the cuisine to be. In other words, there wasn't a ton of garlic being thrown around all the time.

The changes extended beyond the menu. After some deliberating, Sebastian had decided to expand the dining room and install folding glass doors that opened up onto the outdoor dining area modeled almost exactly off of what had burned in the fire. Now, two long tables set with candles and flowers were surrounded by the people we loved most in the world. His entire family had come in for the exclusive reopening of Home, including cousins from out of town who now laughed it up, telling stories and teasing as only family could do. With them were Sebastian's friends and new investors. Even Hadley was there, sitting beside Vaughn's wife, Nova, the two of them deep in girl talk while the guys drank their scotch and busted each other's balls.

The other table was reserved for the staff. Once the dishes were presented, they would feast with us. The additional space meant more help in the kitchen, and we were able to blend the new staff in with the seasoned vets. Lucas was putting the finishing touches on the platters of meat, fish, pasta, and fresh vegetables.

"Everything look okay?" he asked, his gaze moving between Sebastian and me. "You think we're ready to officially open this place?"

Sebastian's hand found mine the way it always tended to do, and the reassuring pressure broke through my inexplicable jitters. It was the first night of something new, the beginning of the future of Home. Our future.

"It looks perfect to me," I decided, and Sebastian agreed with a nod.

A round of applause rose up as we began bringing out the platters and lining them up across the tables. "There's plenty more in the kitchen," Sebastian announced, taking the towel he'd slung over his shoulder and wiping sauce off the edge of a platter of braciole. He just couldn't part with some dishes.

Nonna clapped her hands, beaming. "Such a feast! Oh, I'm glad I saved my appetite." As usual, a plate of calamari was left in front of her, and her eyes gleamed as she snagged a piece.

"Try leaving some for the rest of us, Nonna," Maddie teased before Sebastian tugged her hair in passing. "Knock it off!" she grunted.

"Knock it off with being such a smartass," he retorted, lowering a bowl of fresh pasta onto the table.

Once everything was set up, I hesitated before

taking my seat. It was all perfect—a beautiful, warm night made even more so by the presence of so much laughter. The candles flickered, and the lights strung overhead twinkled. It was the sort of camaraderie that could only exist around a table full of food and filled my soul in a way nothing else could. I was overcome with emotion, almost afraid to move. Like the perfection would be ruined if I did.

"You all right?" Sebastian found me, sliding his arm around my waist. We stood side by side, looking over the results of what we had built *together*.

"Absolutely perfect," I replied with a smile, leaning against him, soaking in the moment before sitting to dig in. "Now don't forget, everybody, we have a lot of dessert waiting too. Save some room."

"Say less," Maddie joked, leaving Sebastian to roll his eyes.

"I would say that was a success."

Sebastian handed me a glass of wine before flopping onto the sofa in his office with a glass of scotch. I had insisted he expand his office during the renovations. It only made sense.

"I still can't believe we got it all done in such a tight timeline," I mused, gazing around the room, thinking back on the night. It was perfect. I ate until I was ready to burst, but it was the laughter and the love that left me smiling hours after everyone cleared out.

Now, it was just the two of us again, reflecting on the night before heading back to his home. *Our home*, where I had already practiced countless new recipes. It was another part of being in love with him—having an actual kitchen at home. The fringe benefits abounded.

Rather than sip the wine, I set it aside in favor of turning toward him. "Everyone seemed so happy tonight. Nonna was so proud of you. I loved looking over at her and seeing her smile when she watched you."

"Did she do that?" A look of fondness washed over his face. "That means everything."

"You mean everything," I told him, leaning over, taking his glass and placing it on the table beside the sofa. I was more interested in crawling into his lap and straddling him, draping my arms around his neck. "You brought all those people together tonight. And you're going to keep doing that every night for years to come. You're such a natural out there, so warm and hospitable. I love you so much."

"Having you next to me makes it all worthwhile," he murmured, his hands sliding up my thighs under my soft, cotton dress. Tonight seemed like an occasion worthy of dressing up for. Now, I was glad it allowed him to touch so much of my skin.

He tasted like scotch and chocolate, which was not a bad combination. Or maybe it was the man himself who woke up my lips along with the rest of me. Maybe it was the taste of him I needed more of, going back for another kiss, then another, pouring all of my love and pride into it because I was proud to be his. I was proud of the life we were building together.

"Are you trying to seduce me, Granger?" he whispered between kisses, his hands moving more deliberately now, stroking my skin, pressing against my flesh. He took my hips and pulled down, pressing me against his growing bulge.

"Since when do I have to try?" I asked, giggling when he rolled his eyes. That didn't stop him from using my body to satisfy his needs.

I invited it because he satisfied my needs, too, and I would never stop needing him.

"It seems like we do it a lot in this building. Have you noticed?" Slowly, I let my dress straps fall from my shoulders, then slid the bodice over my chest and let my breasts fall free. I'd never tire of his reaction—half-lidded eyes and a growl sounding in his throat.

"It makes sense when this is where we spend most of our time," he reasoned, raining soft, tantalizing kisses over the swells of my breasts, lifting them to his lips, teasing my nipples with his tongue. How was it still so electric? So fresh, exciting? It took nothing to light me up to make me wet and needy.

"You are so good at that," I whispered, running my fingers through his hair, pulling his head tight against me. He responded with a groan, using one hand to grab my ass and work me against him. I started moving on my own, grinding, letting the sensations guide me.

"Sweet. So sweet." He kissed his way back up to my throat, lapping at my skin, grazing it with his teeth while I bore down on him when the ache in my pussy turned to demand. I knew what I needed, and I chased it, letting myself get carried away because I knew he would be with me all along the way. I had nothing to fear.

And it was that freedom that let me move faster, harder, humping him like an animal and almost laughing at myself. Joy. There was pure joy in this, in him—his musky, spicy scent, the sound of his groans, and the way his breath heated my skin before his tongue did the same.

"Make yourself come," he growled, gripping my hips with both hands, working with me, his heavy breathing matching my own. Hearing his pleasure intensified mine until I finally felt the familiar tightening, the sense of standing on the edge of a cliff.

And I let myself fall over the edge, flying through space with no fear of hitting the ground.

"Oh, yes," he whispered, holding me in the aftermath, still guiding me slowly against him. "Yes, that's good. Hearing you do that. Watching it come over you. Fucking beautiful."

"Make it happen again," I urged, still hungry, still needy. "Please."

"As if you have to ask." I lifted myself from his lap,

my hands shaking as I opened his belt, then his fly. His sharp gasp at the first touch of my hand turned to a deep, guttural moan once I began to stroke. I wanted him inside me, yes, but I wanted to savor this, too, having him completely under my control, his every breath depending on what I did next. I stared down at him, taking in every muscle twitch, every flare of his nostrils. Watching as he let himself go.

His eyes opened and locked with mine, and my heart swelled until I was sure it would burst. "I love you," he whispered, reaching between my legs to move my thong aside. There was nothing like taking him inside me with nothing between us, feeling his silk-covered steel moving within me.

"Fuck, yes, ride me," he groaned, grabbing my ass, pulling me down on him. "Make yourself come on my cock, baby. I want to feel you squeeze it."

I loved it when he talked like that when he touched my body with so much naked need. "Yes," I whispered as he pulled my head back by my hair so his tongue could run along my throat. "Fuck, yes."

"You like it like that, don't you?" he asked, pulling my head close now, touching his tongue to mine. I moaned into his mouth, moving faster, rocking my hips so my clit could grind against his base. Perfect, so perfect, the pleasure doubling and tripling, radiating through me, turning my body into one giant, throbbing nerve. A pure, sizzling sensation swept me away, enveloping me in the sweetest pleasure.

"Getting tighter," he grunted, and I whimpered my response. "Are you gonna come for me? Is that what you're gonna do?"

"Yes!" I cried, bouncing desperately, losing my rhythm in favor of giving my body what it wanted. *More.* It was all that mattered. *More.*

I came explosively, shattering in his arms, falling against him, and burying my face in his neck while he pumped me up and down a few more times. Slamming me against him one last time, he let go with a deep groan, filling me with a rush of warmth. Perfection. Every last moment.

"You know, there is one good thing about having a sofa in my office." He chuckled against my shoulder before kissing it, still breathing hard.

"What's that?" I asked, sitting up.

"We don't have to sanitize it afterward. You know I'm all about efficiency," he added with a wink that made me laugh. He laughed along with me, touching his forehead to mine before releasing a soft sigh. "I'm all about you."

"Do me a favor and keep it that way, okay?"

"Granger?" He tucked my hair behind my ears, taking my face between his hands. I could never get tired of gazing into his gray eyes. "That is one thing you never have to worry about."

EPILOGUE

GRAYSON

This turn of events was hard to believe. Sitting down to lunch across from a man who, at one time, was closer to me than a brother but was now a stranger. The best friend I ever had when we were kids. "Dominic needs help," Mom had told me during our most recent phone call. "He asked about you. Said he knows you help people for a living."

He knew I never could say no to her. The years had passed, but some things did not change.

Looking at Dominic Garibaldi now, I could hardly believe he was ever the kid I remembered. There was a hardness to him, something in his eyes and the tight set of his mouth that hinted at a life spent doing the sort of shit we tried so hard to understand back in the day. He had lived the way our fathers had. Years of being exposed to the life of a mob captain had formed sort of a shell around him.

Then again, there was a shell around me too. Nobody stayed as innocent as they were when they were kids, no matter what line of work they happened to get into. I made my living wrangling freelance security professionals, digging up intel for Las Vegas movers and shakers, protecting businesses and people who needed help.

He made his living, ensuring people needed protection.

With a sigh, he began. "See, there's a woman."

"There always is," I pointed out with a smirk, which he returned, chuckling softly.

"Yes, and there are always problems, aren't there?" he asked. "In this case, though, she's in trouble. It's my fault."

"What do you mean?"

"She ran off after receiving threats," he explained, releasing a deep breath that seemed to deflate him somewhat. "I have reason to believe members of another family would use her to get to me. She heard something she shouldn't have. They always tell you they'll keep their nose out of your business until curiosity gets the better of them. Then they end up regretting it."

He had a way of making everything sound so official, above board, when we both knew it was anything but. I wondered if he would be more forthcoming if we were alone rather than seated in a restaurant and decided he would not. Silence was golden, always. The less someone revealed, the better for everyone involved.

"Scarlet Bowers. Blackjack dealer." I made a note of this, along with getting a physical description of her—medium height, sandy blonde hair, hazel eyes that leaned more toward green than brown.

"Here, I do have a photo of her." He pulled it up on his phone and placed it on the table for me to see. She was cute with a peaches-and-cream complexion and an ear-to-ear smile. She looked carefree, young, innocent. "I need you to find her for me. From what I understand, you're the man for the job. And you're the only one I trust with something this important. She means a lot, and she's a great girl. She doesn't deserve to live in fear."

I continued studying the photo. *Scarlet Bowers.* A woman who could very well end up roping me back into a world I swore I would never return to.

SAVAGE PROTECTOR

We weren't meant to collide, but the closer we got, the harder it was to resist.

Scarlet

Grayson Daniels is a man I should run from. He's too intense, too dangerous, and when he looks at me, it's like he sees everything I try to hide. I know better than to trust easy promises. But the way he watches me? The way just being near him sets my blood on fire?

He's a threat I can't ignore and maybe, deep down, I don't want to.

Grayson

I thought this would be simple—find Scarlet Bowers, protect her, and walk away. But the moment I laid eyes on her, I knew I was lying to myself. Scarlet is trouble I don't need. She's gorgeous, stubborn, and so damn tempting it wrecks my focus. Every glance, every brush of her skin, pulls me deeper.

This was supposed to be business.

Now, I'm fighting instincts that have nothing to do with duty and everything to do with claiming her.

Get it here:

https://authormissywalker.com/collections/elite-men-of-las-vegas

ACKNOWLEDGMENTS

Growing up with Sicilian grandparents food was the epicentre of our home. Love, family, arguments, laughter — it all happened around the table. I spent countless mornings at my grandparents' house, starting prep early, whether I liked it or not!

Everything was handmade. Everything took forever.

At ten years old, being stuck crumbing, stuffing and rolling meats felt like actual torture. Especially when I made a tiny mistake and my Nonna always made me do it again. But it was always worth it when it was finally time to eat. The food was always chef's kiss. And yes, you'd think all that time in the kitchen would've turned me into a master chef. Spoiler, it didn't.

What it did give me were memories. Real ones. Of good, honest food. Simple food. The kind that doesn't need dressing up to be unforgettable.

Nonna would spend six hours in the kitchen without a single complaint, cooking for the whole family on a tiny, barely-hanging-on stove. She was a machine. Fierce, fiery as hell, but gentle where it mattered. She fed everyone before herself and loved with her whole body.

This story grew from that place — the hunger, the desire, the fire. Claudia's strength and Sebastian's devotion were shaped by my Nonna's spirit. Every page carries a piece of her. I hope you feel her in these pages, because I felt her every time I wrote them.

Finally, thank you to my editors for your sharp eyes, honesty, and care in shaping this story into what it became. And to my beta readers — thank you for reading early, feeling deeply, and reminding me why telling these stories matters.

Stay Fabulous,

Missy x

JOIN MISSY'S CLUB

Hear about exclusive book releases, teasers, discounts and book bundles before anyone else.

Sign up to Missy's newsletter here:
www.authormissywalker.com

Become part of Missy's Facebook Reader Group where we chat all things books, releases and of course fun giveaways!

https://www.facebook.com/groups/missywalkersbookbabes

ABOUT THE AUTHOR

Missy is an Australian author who writes kissing books with equal parts angst and steam. Stories about billionaires, forbidden romance, and second chances roll around in her mind probably more than they ought to.

When she's not writing, she's taking care of her two daughters and doting husband and conjuring up her next saucy plot.

Inspired by the acreage she lives on, Missy regularly distracts herself by visiting her orchard, baking naughty but delicious foods, and socialising with her girl squad.

Then there's her overweight cat—Charlie, chickens, and border collie dog—Benji if she needed another excuse to pass the time.

If you like Missy Walker's books, consider leaving a review and following her here:

instagram.com/missywalkerauthor
facebook.com/AuthorMissyWalker
tiktok.com/@authormissywalker
bookbub.com/profile/missy-walker

ALSO BY MISSY WALKER

Elite men of Las Vegas - Coming 2026

Sinfully Bound

Burning Rivalry

Savage Protector

Buried Truths

Stolen Kiss

Final Vow

Elite men of Los Angeles

Scarred Heart

Broken Rules

Reluctantly Yours

Entangled Vow

Velvet Sin

Boundless Love

Elite Men of Manhattan

Forbidden Lust*

Forbidden Love*

Lost Love

Missing Love

Guarded Love

Infinite Love Novella

Elite Heirs of Manhattan

Seductive Hearts

Sweet Surrender

Sinful Desires

Silent Cravings

Sensual Games

Endless Love

Elite Mafia of New York Series

Cruel Lust*

Stolen Love

Finding Love

Slater Siblings Series

Hungry Heart

Chained Heart

Iron Heart

Small Town Desires Series

Trusting the Rockstar

Trusting the Ex

Trusting the Player

*Forbidden Lust/Love are a duet and to be read in order.

*Cruel Lust, Stolen Love and Finding Love are a trilogy and to be read in order.

All other books are stand alones.

www.ingramcontent.com/pod-product-compliance
Lightning Source LLC
Chambersburg PA
CBHW050757080726
47590CB00020B/202

* 9 7 8 1 9 2 3 0 3 6 4 2 0 *